THE ETHICS OF EUTHANASIA

Other Books in the At Issue Series:

THE ETHICS OF EUTHANASIA

Daniel A. Leone, *Book Editor*

David Bender, *Publisher*
Bruno Leone, *Executive Editor*

Bonnie Szumski, *Editorial Director*
Brenda Stalcup, *Managing Editor*
Scott Barbour, *Senior Editor*

An Opposing Viewpoints® Series

Greenhaven Press, Inc.
San Diego, California

Library of Congress Cataloging-in-Publication Data

The ethics of euthanasia / Daniel A. Leone, book editor.
       p.   cm. — (At issue) (An opposing viewpoints series)
    Includes bibliographical references and index.
    ISBN 0-7377-0005-X (lib. bdg. : alk. paper). —
ISBN 0-7377-0004-1 (pbk. : alk. paper)
    1. Euthanasia—Moral and ethical aspects. 2. Terminal care—
Moral and ethical aspects. 3. Life support systems (Critical care)—
Moral and ethical aspects. 4. Right to die. I. Leone, Daniel A.,
1969–   . II. Series: At issue (San Diego, Calif.) III. Series:
Opposing viewpoints series (Unnumbered)
R726.E7753   1999
179.7—dc21   98-36587
                                                          CIP

© 1999 by Greenhaven Press, Inc., PO Box 289009,
San Diego, CA 92198-9009

Printed in the U.S.A.

Every effort has been made to trace owners of copyrighted material.

Table of Contents

Introduction

On June 5, 1998, United States attorney general Janet Reno declared that doctors who prescribed lethal medicine to terminally ill patients would not be prosecuted. The decision overturned a Drug Enforcement Agency (DEA) policy statement that had been issued in November of that year without her approval. The DEA policy stated that using drugs to commit suicide is not permitted under federal drug laws and that the United States government would impose severe penalties on any doctor who prescribed lethal drugs to patients. By overruling the DEA, Reno eliminated the last legal barrier to the implementation of the controversial Oregon assisted-suicide law. Oregon State's Death with Dignity Act, which had been passed by voters in 1994 but had been blocked by federal legal challenges ever since, permits terminally ill patients to request lethal drugs to hasten their death—provided they are mentally competent and considered by two doctors to have less than six months to live.

Prior to Reno's decision, the Supreme Court had ruled on June 26, 1997, that there is no constitutionally protected "right to die." The Court's decision overturned two earlier U.S. courts of appeals rulings. In *Washington State vs. Glucksberg,* the Ninth Circuit court had ruled that Washington State's law prohibiting assisted suicide was unconstitutional. The court had concluded that the right to control the manner and timing of one's death is protected under the Fourteenth Amendment. In *New York vs. Quill,* the Second Circuit court had ruled similarly that a New York State law prohibiting individuals from aiding in suicides was unconstitutional. In both cases, the courts' decisions recognized a constitutionally protected right to die.

In effect, the attorney general's and Supreme Court's decisions ensured that the seemingly endless controversy and debates surrounding euthanasia and assisted suicide would continue. Although the Court decided against a constitutionally protected right to die, it also noted that neither its decision nor the Constitution have absolute power over the states. Individual states remain free to create their own legislation regarding the right to die and assisting in a suicide. Furthermore, the Court implied that state laws prohibiting assisted suicide may still be challenged in the future. Reno noted in her decision that the act of euthanasia involves complex moral and ethical considerations and that the government never intended for the DEA to attempt to resolve or intrude on such delicate matters. Essentially, the two decisions made by the federal government shifted the responsibility of legislating assisted suicide to the states. According to legal experts and commentators, it is only a matter of time before additional states enact euthanasia laws and, consequently, ignite another series of legal battles and ethical debates.

Euthanasia is defined as the act of killing for reasons of mercy. While all acts of euthanasia involve the hastening of death, not all acts are identical. Several terms have been coined to describe different types of euthanasia. Voluntary and involuntary euthanasia, passive and active euthanasia, assisted suicide, and physician-assisted suicide are terms regularly used to label specific acts. Assisted suicide takes place when an individual wishing to hasten his or her death requests help to carry out the act. Physician-assisted suicide differs from assisted suicide in that the individual wishing to die requests the support of their doctor as opposed to a family member or friend. The important distinction between assisted suicide and other types of euthanasia is that during an assisted suicide the dying person asks for death and is completely aware of the procedure. On the other hand, involuntary euthanasia is the act of causing the death of an individual without their consent. A husband's withdrawing a life-support system from his unconscious wife, causing her immediate death, is an example of involuntary euthanasia because the wife is unaware that her life is being ended. Conversely, if the wife were conscious, and if she and her husband both agreed that he should withdraw her life support system, he would be committing an act of voluntary euthanasia because the wife is aware and approves of the termination of her life.

While the terms voluntary and involuntary euthanasia are used to describe the dying person's level of awareness, passive and active euthanasia distinguish between the method used to end a life. Active euthanasia occurs when a person actually takes the life of a suffering or dying individual instead of allowing them to die from natural causes. Giving a lethal injection to a friend who is dying of cancer is an act of active euthanasia. Passive euthanasia takes place when life-sustaining treatment is withdrawn and a person is allowed to die from their disease or injury. Today, most people agree that passive euthanasia is ethically acceptable. In 1976, the New Jersey Supreme Court, in the case of Karen Ann Quinlan, established the constitutional right of a patient to refuse treatment. In 1975, after a drug overdose, Quinlan had fallen into what her doctors judged to be an irreversible coma and was kept alive by a life-support system. Her parents' request that she be disconnected from the life-support system and allowed to die was denied, forcing them to pursue legal channels. The court decided in favor of Quinlan's parents and created a legal precedent for passive euthanasia. The court emphasized the distinction between passive and active euthanasia, stressing that while a person now had the right to refuse treatment, that did not entitle them to receive assistance in committing suicide or active euthanasia. Today, active euthanasia is still illegal and controversial.

Ethical distinctions between passive and active euthanasia

There has been tremendous controversy and debate over whether ethical distinctions exist between passive and active euthanasia. Some ethics experts contend that it is ethically irrelevant whether a doctor withdraws treatment or gives a lethal injection to end a patient's life because in either case the doctor's intention is to terminate that life. Therefore, they argue, if it is morally permissible to withdraw treatment to terminate a life, then it should be equally acceptable to inject a patient with a lethal dose to accomplish the same objective. As expressed by Tom Beauchamp, a senior research scholar at the Kennedy Institute of Ethics, "The justification for assistance in bringing about death in medicine is an extension of the justification for letting patients die. Letting a patient die by accepting a valid refusal to continue in life is directly analogous to helping a patient die by accepting a valid request for help."

Others contend that there is an ethical distinction between passive and active euthanasia that must always be recognized. They argue that the act of medical intervention that purposely hastens death clearly carries a different ethical responsibility than an act of withdrawing treatment to allow death to come about naturally. E.J. Dionne Jr., a columnist for the *Washington Post,* writes, "It is a terrible leap to declare that withdrawing support is exactly the same as helping a patient commit suicide. In the first case, we are acknowledging that great medical advances permit us to trump nature and keep people alive long after they would otherwise have died. In the second, we are taking active measures to kill." Opponents of active euthanasia are concerned that if the act is legalized and practiced regularly, many vulnerable patients will be pressured into choosing assisted death by greedy health insurers trying to cut costs or even by family members who think they know what is best for their terminally ill loved one. Critics fear that this will inevitably lead society down the "slippery slope" to widespread involuntary euthanasia of the retarded, elderly, or any others judged to have a life not worth living.

Euthanasia is an extremely sensitive and emotionally laden topic. Rarely does an issue spark such intense and complex discussions based on ethics and morality. This anthology, *At Issue: The Ethics of Euthanasia,* examines the ethical concerns of euthanasia from medical, religious, and academic perspectives.

1

Euthanasia Can Be Ethical

Arthur Rifkin

Arthur Rifkin is a professor of psychiatry at the Albert Einstein College of Medicine.

While many terminally ill patients can indefinitely relieve their suffering through the use of effective pain management techniques, there are some patients whose pain cannot be mitigated. Rather than endure great pain and suffering for the remainder of their life, these patients should have the ethical choice to end their lives. Despite justifiable concern over the potential abuse of euthanasia and assisted suicide, competent patients who are suffering should not be denied the option of assisted death.

P hysician-assisted suicide in a concrete fashion forces us to consider and act on what we consider ultimate. It not only makes us question whether someone should commit suicide, but whether another person should help.

Do we "play God" when we seek to end life? The typical instance concerns someone terminally ill who considers life meaningless because of pain and mental and physical impediments. Technology, as in many areas, creates advantages and disadvantages. We live longer and more comfortably because of medical advances, such as renal dialysis, organ transplantations, joint replacement, and antidepressants. But technology, as well, can simply prolong dying. Where pneumonia, "the old man's friend," would kill a debilitated person relatively quickly, we, often, can prevent this. Mechanical ventilation and parenteral nutrition extend life, even for long periods of unconsciousness or stupor.

We can reduce suffering. Optimal treatment of pain can remove much discomfort, although many patients don't receive optimal pain management because of the mistaken concern that tolerance will develop to the analgesic effect or worry about addiction. Much suffering comes from unkind treatment, from insensitive care-givers, neglect from family and friends, and unpleasant surroundings. Much suffering comes from the narrowing of areas that sustain interest and pleasure, by sensory loss, invalidism, and lack of intellectual and social opportunities. Compassionate, intelligent care in pleasant surroundings would alleviate much suffering.

Reprinted from Arthur Rifkin, "Spiritual Aspects of Physician-Assisted Suicide," *Friends Journal*, October 1997, by permission of the author and *Friends Journal*.

However, for many people we cannot mitigate the suffering. We think unrealistically if we expect to make all dying free of severe suffering.

The situation is not hopeless: some very painful conditions remit, even if the patient does not recognize that this can occur. This raises the very difficult question of determining if the dying person has the mental capacity to make the decision to end his or her life. We would not honor the decision to commit suicide by minors or people with mental disorders, which includes everything from alcohol intoxication to Alzheimer's Disease. The difficult issue is assessing depression. We rightly protect a depressed person from committing suicide because his or her judgement is impaired, and most depressions eventually lift.

How do we distinguish depression from existential despair in the dying?

For many people we cannot mitigate the suffering.

If the dying person no longer enjoys usual activities, has a poor appetite, sleeps poorly, cannot concentrate well, feels hopeless, and wants to die, are these symptoms of a mental disorder (depression) or understandable and reasonable responses to the illness and its treatment, and/or the result of the illness or treatment? Can we make the case for a mental disorder? Do the symptoms hang together, are the course, family history, and response to treatment predictable? Several studies have shown that depression associated with physical illness does respond to antidepressant drugs, but no studies have included terminally ill patients.

Some psychiatrists aver that the wish to die in a terminally ill patient always represents a treatable mental disorder if not depression then demoralization—a sense of unrealistic pessimism. This assumes that the realistic suffering of dying can be ameliorated, a questionable assumption.

As I assess the situation, there are inadequate psychiatric reasons for considering all instances of suicidal desires instances of psychopathology, and we cannot ameliorate all terrible suffering and lack of dignity in dying persons, although we can do a lot more than we have. The hospice movement shows that much can be done.

Do we play God by terminating a natural process? I think not. We hardly live in some pure state of nature. In small and large ways we don't "let nature take its course." We foster death by many unhealthful practices. We forestall death by healthful living, environment changes, and medical treatment.

Most people, and all courts, recognize that patients can request discontinuation of life support measures. Do we cross some qualitative bridge between ending life support measures and assisting in suicide, or is this more a quantitative difference, or is it no difference? It seems very late in the day to concern ourselves with altering nature. For better or worse, we have grasped the helm of much that determines our lives. It seems like cowardice and hypocrisy to lift our hands away from the rudder and say, "Now God, you take over."

Is opposition to physician-assisted suicide the last gasp of the "God of the gaps," pinning on God what we remain ignorant of, namely how to make our deaths a deeply spiritually meaningful event and not horrendous torture we would never think of inflicting on anyone? Does it serve God's purpose for us to lose, at the ends of our lives, that which characterizes us at our spiritual best: intentionality, seeking the Light Within to lead us to our culmination? This should be our time of letting go and deepest insight, not a time of agony, stupor, undignified dependence, a prisoner of tighter restrictions than inmates of a maximum security prison endure. Must we become slaves to our failing bodies?

The 22nd Psalm aptly describes a horrible death:

> I am poured out like water,
> and all my bones are out of joint;
> my heart is like wax;
> it is melted within my breast;
> my mouth is dried up like a potsherd,
> and my tongue sticks to my jaws;
> you lay me in the dust of death.

This psalm then leads to the magnificent, stately 23rd, filled with peaceful gratitude:

> Even though I walk through the darkest
> valley,
> I fear no evil;
> for you are with me;
> your rod and your staff,
> they comfort me.

Is it stretching too far to say that the shepherd's rod at the time of death could be the physician's lethal dose of medication?

Safeguards and the slippery slope

A treatment of ultimate finality—physician-assisted suicide—must have the most stringent safeguards against misuse. Although distinguishing reversible depression from nonreversible existential anguish is difficult, psychiatrists should use care to recognize and treat reversible depression. We should try to create an ambience most conducive to a meaningful death. We should have a method of paying for healthcare that does not drain away remaining resources. We should provide caretakers who view it as a privilege to competently and compassionately use technical skills and understanding to assist the dying patient.

We should not permit our hubris of thinking we can overcome the suffering of dying to keep the physician from acceding to the patient's request for a lethal dose. We hear misguided claims that following the Hippocratic Oath would keep physicians from assisting in suicide. The spirit of the Hippocratic Oath says the physician should be devoted to the patient's interests. How we define those interests today should not be limited by our understanding of medicine over two millennia ago.

What of the slippery slope? Does physician-assisted suicide open the door to unethical practices of killing people without consent and without good cause? The answer to unintelligent, unscrupulous behavior is intelligence and scrupulous concern for the patient's interest and not manacles to prevent ethical, useful acts. The history of humankind is a widening circle of compassionate and just concerns. We have recognized the need to free ourselves from the injustice of slavery, mistreatment of children, unequal treatment of women, and ethnic and religious bigotry. Now the horizon of concern has reached a group often treated as unfairly and sadistically as any of the foregoing groups: the dying. Let us grasp the chance boldly.

2

Euthanasia Can
Never Be Justified

J. Budziszewski

J. Budziszewski is an associate professor in the departments of government and philosophy at the University of Texas at Austin.

Supporters attempt to justify euthanasia on the grounds that it is done with good intentions. However, there is a fallacy in this argument; to kill oneself or someone else is wrong, regardless of the motivation or circumstances. Rather than being motivated by good intentions, attempts to defend euthanasia are founded on corrupt values. Society must strive to understand why euthanasia is wrong and why it cannot be justified by good intentions.

Historians will write that by the last decade of the twentieth century, great numbers of men and women in the most pampered society on the earth had come to think it normal and desirable that their sick, their weak, and their helpless should be killed. When they were a poor country, they had not so thought; now in the day of their power and prosperity, they changed their minds. Babies asleep in the dim of the womb were awakened by knife-edged cannulas that sucked and tore at their soft young limbs; white-haloed grandmothers with wandering minds were herded by white-smocked shepherds into the cold dark waters of death. Many physicians came to think of suicide as though it were a medicine.

How is it even possible to think such thoughts? How can so many of our neighbors have been persuaded of their truth? How can a mind entertain the goodness of evil for as much as a moment without curling up and returning to dust? The paradox is as sharp as a broken bone, for it is not as though the people of our place and time have ceased thinking of what is right and good. That is not even a possibility for human minds. No, our neighbors tell themselves that they are *doing* the right and good. Therein lies the mystery.

There is a rule for probing such mysteries. We may call it the Asymmetry Principle, for it holds that one can only understand the bad from the good, not the good from the bad. Do we want to know how it is pos-

Reprinted from J. Budziszewski, "Why We Kill the Weak," *Human Life Review*, Fall 1997, by permission of the author and the *Human Life Review*.

sible to be foul? Then we have to know how it is possible to be fair. Have we need to fathom the spreading desire to kill all those who have the greatest claim on our protection? Then we must fathom the good impulses from whose pollution this bad one comes.

In Augustine's day, the Manichaeans proposed a different principle. In their view, evil did not require any special explanation because it was one of the primordial realities. There are good things like light, health, and virtue, and there are bad things like darkness, disease, and sin. Both have existed from the beginning; a good deity created all the former, and a bad deity created all the latter. That's all.

Although the Manichaean view seems simpler, it cannot be true. Everything bad is just a good thing spoiled. I can block the light in order to cast shadow pictures on the wall, but I cannot block the dark in order to cast bright ones. I can ruin a man's health to make him sick, but I cannot ruin his sickness to make him well. The veriest devil must possess the goods of existence, intelligence, power, and will; they become evil only through their disordered condition. Augustine taught us this.

What then are those goods whose pollution produces the wish to destroy the weak? Perhaps the most important are pity, prudence, amenity, honor, remorse, love, and the sense of justice. Let's consider how each in turn is spoiled.

Spoiled pity. In his ruminations on the original condition of mankind, Jean-Jacques Rousseau called pity an innate repugnance to see one's fellow suffer. Even animals have it, he said, for cattle low upon entering a slaughterhouse and a horse does not willingly pass near a corpse. The idea seems to be that the sight of pain makes me feel pain myself, and I don't like it. My pity is ultimately self-regarding.

This definition rather misses the point. True pity is a heartfelt sorrow for the suffering of another, seen or not, moving us to render what aid we can. True, there may be something self-regarding in pity—by rendering aid, I do alleviate the pain I feel as a witness—but my focus is on the pain of the other. By contrast, in Rousseauistic "pity" the self-regarding element has taken over. Yes, rendering aid to the other would alleviate my pain; but if there is an easier way to escape the terrible spectacle, then from a Rousseauistic point of view, so much the better. I can run away; I can turn my back; I can close my eyes. Perhaps that is why Rousseau left all his own children at orphanages.

Many physicians came to think of suicide as though it were a medicine.

But though Rousseau's definition fails dismally for true pity, for spoiled pity it works perfectly well. The purpose of pity is to prime the pump of loving kindness, but when we refuse to use it in that way the impulse is merely displaced. While in true pity we move closer to the sufferer, in degraded pity we move farther away. While in true pity we try to change the painful sight, in degraded pity we merely try to make it go away. And there are lots of ways to do that.

Then again maybe there aren't. In a society like ours, with no more frontier and hardly enough room to turn around, killing the sufferer may well be the cheapest and easiest way of making the painful sight go away. As someone said in the case of George Delury, imprisoned for poisoning and suffocating his sick wife, I may say I am putting her out of her misery, but I am really putting her out of mine.

Spoiled prudence. Some things and persons must be entrusted to my care, and others to yours. Wiser than Marx, even Plato proposed communism only with tongue in cheek; he laughed about it and admitted that it would never work. Not caring even for the joke, Aristotle taught that when things are held in common they are not well cared for. We need homes, not warrens, families, not orphanages, and belongings, not tribal hordes. In the eyes of God my young children, my ancient parents, and my personal affairs are not really mine; I have merely been made a caretaker of them. But that standard is too high for the law, which must accommodate itself to the fact of sin—including the sin of busybodiness. It may be fashionable to say that it takes a whole village to raise a child—and it is certainly true that parents need to support each other—but a wiser proverb is that with the whole village *kibitzing* I cannot properly take care of anyone or anything.

Killing the sufferer may well be the cheapest and easiest way of making the painful sight go away.

Prudence, then, is good judgment and conscientious care for the things and the persons entrusted to me. We may call it the insight and impulse of responsible stewardship.

Perhaps it isn't hard to see how the legal standard is confused with the moral norm—how stewardship decays into ownership. I come to think that my life, my affairs, and my relatives really are mine, mine in the ultimate sense, and that I may do with them as I please. After this, just one little step takes me to the sheer urge to control. The urge is bad, but we can never understand it if we think of it as *simply* bad. Consider, for example, how hard it is to shame people who insist on control. They don't merely resist; they become indignant, morally indignant, as though someone were interfering with their virtue. Why is this? Because the bad impulse to be in control is parasitic on the good impulse to exercise responsible stewardship—an impulse which has its own proper place in the order of things and its own proper claim on the conscience.

Spoiled prudence, then, manifests itself in the notion that I have the *right* to protect my life from the distractions of your suffering and dependence, and the right to manipulate you in the manner most convenient to me. These notions make strange bedfellows: the modern feminist agrees with the ancient Roman father that children are merely an extension of one's body, and the Dutch agree with the Eskimos that the old have a duty to get out of the way. But we should not be surprised. If the potentiality for prudence is universal, then the potentiality for its corruption must be universal too.

Spoiled amenity. Amenity, or complaisance, is the impulse every person has to accommodate himself to all others. Like every moral impulse it carries sanctions: in this case, fear of rejection and desire to belong. But as with every moral impulse, the sanctions are only training wheels, preparing us for obedience to a deeper moral principle written on the heart. A mature person accommodates himself to others not just from fear of rejection and the desire to belong, but from concern for their legitimate interests.

The problem, of course, is that in many of us the impulse never does mature. We continue to rely on the training wheels and never learn to ride. Unfortunately, this makes a difference. Mature amenity draws a boundary; precisely because I care about the legitimate interests of others, my willingness to accommodate has a limit. At just the point where going along would not be good for all, I call a halt. Stunted amenity cannot make such distinctions. It cannot stop accommodating; it doesn't know how. I give Grandma lethal drugs to accommodate my relatives; to accommodate me, Grandma asks for lethal drugs. A girl has an abortion to accommodate her boyfriend; to accommodate his girlfriend, the boy goes along. We know these things are wrong, but for fear of being on the outs with others we do them anyway. In the extreme case, we accommodate each other to death.

Of course people suffer remorse when they commit these terrible deeds. For present purposes, the more interesting fact is that they also tend to suffer remorse when they refuse to commit them. When they hold out, when they say no, when they resist the clamor of voices telling them what to do, they feel not only afraid, but *in the wrong*. This shows that, like prudence, the urge to accommodate is not *simply* self-regard even when it is spoiled and self-regarding. It draws strength from the very sense of obligation that it corrupts. Conscience always does the best it can; when driven from its proper course, it finds another course and flows on.

Spoiled honor. To honor someone is to show him the reverence due to him as a fellow image of God, distinct from myself, sent into the world for the Creator's pleasure, not my own. The impulse to honor others is the best vaccine against the urge to control them, but it suffers from corruptions of its own.

> *The Dutch agree with the Eskimos that the old have a duty to get out of the way.*

In one case within my own experience, a woman tried to honor her husband by sparing him what she thought would be a dreadful ordeal. "If I ever become a burden to you," she said, "I want you to pull the plug." Although this was not to his liking at all, he tried to honor her in turn by giving her his promise in return. Before considering the outcome, let's consider what was wrong with the deeds.

What spoiled the woman's attempt to honor her husband was that she did not treat him as a moral being. Had he become helpless she would have borne any burden to care for him; she demeaned him by thinking that he needed to be spared bearing burdens to care for her. What she thought was honoring him violated the Golden Rule, for she would not allow him to do for her what *she* would have wanted to do, had she been in his place.

What spoiled the husband's attempt to honor his wife was that he made her an illicit promise. He forgot that it is impossible to reverence the image of God in another by complying with what soils that image. Had *he* expressed an immoral wish, he would have wanted her to challenge him; yet when she expressed an immoral wish, he would not challenge her. So he violated the Golden Rule too.

The outcome? She did, in time, become sick and dependent, and she wanted him, for his sake, to keep his promise. In an unseemly rush, not wanting to but believing he had to, he did. She died, he grieved most terribly—and he found himself unable to stop. The trauma of her death was overwhelmed by the trauma of his killing her. To the end of his own life, many years later, remorse made each day like the day that her heart had stopped. With the thought of sparing him a burden that he could have borne, she had thrust on him another burden that he could not bear. With the thought of complying with her wish, he had made that burden his own. Trapped by spoiled honor on every side, he did not even know how to repent.

I give Grandma lethal drugs to accommodate my relatives.

Spoiled remorse. Guilt is an objective reality—the condition of being in violation of moral law. By contrast, remorse is a subjective reality—the *feeling* of being in violation of moral law. What is the purpose of the feeling? Obviously, to prod us into recognition of objective guilt so that we can repent and throw ourselves upon the mercy of God.

It may seem strange that remorse could ever get us *into* trouble, instead of out of it. On the contrary, nothing is more common. Like every moral impulse, remorse can be displaced. It can refuse the relief of repentance and seek alleviation in another way instead. In the short term, remorse can even be palliated by further wrongdoing. The first murder in history was undertaken from spoiled remorse. Cain's sacrifice had been unacceptable to God; he killed his righteous brother to get rid of the reminder of his shame.

In another article I related several stories of women who had abortions because of remorse over previous abortions. There was the woman who was afraid God would "do something" to the new baby to punish her for killing the other, so she beat Him to the punch. And there was the woman who had her first abortion out of anger because her husband had been unfaithful to her, and her second because "I wanted to be able to hate myself more for what I did to the first baby." In much the same way that some people use one credit card to pay off another, she was trying to abate her present remorse by increasing her burden of future remorse.

We may be sure that spoiled remorse is just as great a motive for killing the sick and the old. For years, perhaps, I have neglected my aging father. Now, when he is weak and dependent, the burden of my conscience has become intolerable. I cannot bear the reproach of his watery eyes; I would rather endure the blows of his fists than the sight of his withered hands. To avoid him I visit him less and less. One day he requires hospitalization and cannot feed himself. He is not dying, he is not unconscious, he is not even in great discomfort; nevertheless I tell his caretakers to withdraw his food and water. It is easier to face them than to face him, for he is the sole surviving witness to the slights of his ungrateful son. Besides, I tell myself, I no longer deserve a father. When his body is buried, perhaps my guilt will be buried too.

Spoiled love. Love is a perfect determination of the will to further the true good of another person. As such, it can miss the mark in either of two different ways. If the will is unsteady, then we call the love weak; if the understanding is bent, then we call the love spoiled. The faults of weak love are faults of omission, in that I fail to care sufficiently for the one who needs my mercy. But the faults of spoiled love are faults of commission, in that I may actually do him harm.

Although the modes of spoiled love are infinite in number, it may suffice to mention two. In one mode, what stunts my charity is a failure to understand the involvement of each human being in all the others. Many of us have known parents who have abortions for the sake of a child already born. They honestly believe that Johnny is an island, entire to himself; that it will be better for him if Sally is cut in pieces before her birth, because with one less child their home will be quieter and their finances more secure. In this frame of mind, Grandma too seems a threat to the younger members of the family. Isn't she just a useless eater? Up there in her nursing home she merely consumes while giving nothing back. Of course I don't mind spending time and money on her *myself*—after all, she *is* my mother—but why must my *child* do with less?

It is difficult to explain the wrong of abortion to someone who thinks it is better for Johnny to have a trip to Disney World than a baby sister, difficult to explain the wrong of euthanasia to one who thinks he will be more blessed learning to take than to sacrifice for a lady who needs his mercy.

> *She demeaned him by thinking that he needed to be spared bearing burdens to care for her.*

In the other mode of spoiled love, what stunts my charity is a failure to understand the good of affliction. "Truly . . . affliction is a treasure," says John Donne, "and scarce any man hath enough of it." Of course, no one should seek affliction or gratuitously impose it on another, but is there a soul alive who has not learned more from his hard times than his good? How dare we then imagine that our dear ones are like animals who, when they suffer, have nothing to learn from it, and are fit only to be "put out of their misery"? What arrogance is it that denies to the sick at the last that teacher to which each of us is most indebted?

But this is an even harder lesson than the last one. That for fallen natures, physical suffering may sometimes accomplish moral good is a fact of everyday experience, but for people who do not even believe in spanking it may be hard to teach.

The spoiled sense of justice. The sense of justice is the desire to see that each is given his due—that the good are rewarded and the bad are punished. It isn't hard to see how a spoiled sense of justice can make me feel justified in mistreating someone weak who I think has hurt me in the past.

Perhaps I nurse a grievance against my parents for wrongs done to me when they were large and strong and I was small and weak; now the tables are turned and I finally have the chance to pay them out. Perhaps they didn't really wrong me but I think they did; my generation has been more indulged, and consequently has a stronger sense of grievance, than any other in history. Of course resentment is an unpleasant feeling, but if I can convert it into moral indignation I feel much better.

The main problem is that all *wrongs are done from good motives.*

Even more alarming is the tendency of the guilty conscience to call spoiled justice to its aid by *inventing* grievances. Cause and effect here trade places: We think of resentment coming first and mistreatment coming after, but it is often the other way around. People almost always resent the people they have treated worst, as a defense against the shame of having treated them so poorly in the first place. Unfortunately, such effects take on a life of their own and become real *causes*. Having invented a grievance to justify my neglect, I may now act in malice at the prompting of the grievance. I may resent my father for no reason other than I have mistreated him; nevertheless, having invented a fictitious reason for mistreating him, I now feel justified in wanting him to die.

Not that I am likely to be so honest with myself about my thoughts. I may not admit my resentment at all, because we do not call it "just" to kick a man when he is down. But my secret sense of grievance will always be a finger on the scale of my benevolence, biasing me toward what anyone but myself would recognize as spite.

There is a fallacy in our judgments about these things. It results from a distinction we ought not make. Some wrongdoing, we say, should be treated with lenity because it is committed with good motives. Other wrongdoing, we say, should be treated harshly because it is committed with bad ones. She killed her sick father out of desire for his inheritance, so she should be judged; he killed his sick mother out of sympathy for her pain, so he should be pardoned. She had an abortion because her exams were coming up, so she should be condemned; he supported the abortion out of respect for her decision, so he should be excused.

Distinguishing among motives is often no more than a way to let ourselves off the hook while keeping the others on it. After all, we know our own motives much better than we can ever know theirs; therefore we know the good in our motives much better than the good in theirs. We are always in a better position to plead extenuating circumstances in *our* case.

But that is not the main problem with pardoning wrongs that are done from good motives. The main problem is that *all* wrongs are done from good motives. As we said at the beginning, there is no such thing as pure or perfect evil; every bad thing is a good thing spoiled. Without good motives to corrupt, there could be no wrongdoing at all. Did George Delury kill his wife because he hated the sight of her suffering? Then the motive was spoiled pity. Did he do it to stay in control? Then it was spoiled prudence. To go along with her wishes? Spoiled amenity. To keep a promise? Spoiled honor. To bury his shame, to put her out of her misery, to pay her back for hurting him? Spoiled remorse, spoiled love, spoiled sense of justice. That the raw material of his intention was *good* was the condition of his having an intention at all. But that he *ruined* that good material through a free exercise of his will was what made the intention evil.

To understand all wrong is not to excuse all wrong; rather, to understand it is to know why it is wrong. Yet achieving such understanding is far from useless. From the throne of mercy there may yet be mercy for a merciless generation, but not before we know what we have done. We had best get started, for we have done a great deal.

3

Patients' Wishes Regarding Euthanasia Should Be Respected

Peter B. Terry and Karen A. Korzick

Peter B. Terry is a professor of medicine in the Division of Pulmonary and Critical Care Medicine at Johns Hopkins University in Baltimore, Maryland. Karen A. Korzick is a fellow in the Division of Pulmonary and Critical Care Medicine at Johns Hopkins University.

There is a general consensus that physicians and patients should communicate directly about end-of-life preferences and decisions. However, studies indicate that many physicians do not initiate such discussions or accept the responsibility for doing so. This reluctance by physicians to approach their patients on such matters has been attributed to physicians' ethical and legal concerns regarding euthanasia. In addition, many physicians cite a general lack of knowledge on how to appropriately manage such a delicate and sensitive situation. As a result, many patients' wishes regarding end-of-life decisions are not understood or are even disregarded by physicians or family members. Physicians should respect and honor the patients' wishes on end-of-life issues.

Editor's note: The following viewpoint was written in response to JoAnn Bell Reckling's article "Withholding and Withdrawing Life-Sustaining Treatment?" which appeared in the spring 1997 issue of the Journal of Clinical Ethics.

End-of-life decision making encompasses several topics that have received increased attention over the past decade from medical professionals, bioethicists, the law, patients, and society. These topics include withdrawal of care, do-not-resuscitate (DNR) orders, euthanasia, and assisted suicide. Closely related topics such as futility, utilization of resources, and cost-containment have also been considered in these discussions. As might be predicted when considering issues of great complexity within the milieu of modern society, few points of consensus have been reached. However, a consensus does seem to exist on one point: doctors and patients should talk about end-of-life decisions.

While consensus exists that doctors and patients should hold these discussions, there is lack of consensus on several key points. What roles should healthcare providers, patients, and their family members have in these discussions? How should conflicts be resolved? How often should decisions be re-evaluated? How can an increase in the frequency with which these discussions occur be achieved? Which bioethical principles, if any, should guide clinical decision making?

In her article, JoAnn Bell Reckling examines the roles played by healthcare providers and patients' family members during discussions about withholding and withdrawing life-sustaining treatment. She makes several observations that are interesting and deserve further comment.

The role of physicians

First, she notes that in all 10 patients studied, a physician initiated the discussion. This was interpreted as being related to "the apparent acceptance of this responsibility as a part of a physician's professional role." While we agree that in certain instances the responsibility for initiating these discussions belongs to the patient's physician, there is evidence that physicians as a whole do not accept this responsibility. The SUPPORT Study documented that physicians did not routinely query their patients about end-of-life decisions, and that they did not respond to interventions that had been designed to increase the frequency with which these discussions were held.[1] Physicians' reluctance to discuss end-of-life decision making has been documented in other studies.[2] Multiple explanations have been given, including a lack of knowledge about end-of-life decision-making techniques, perceived threats to physicians' autonomy by including patients in the decision-making process, fear that a DNR order is frequently interpreted by nursing staff and house officers to mean "do not treat anything anymore," fear of legal consequences if care is withheld or withdrawn, time constraints, belief that these discussions upset patients, and personal beliefs held by physicians with regard to end-of-life decisions. Just as there have been many reasons cited for physicians' failure to initiate such discussions, there have been numerous suggestions for ways to motivate physicians to improve their behavior. These range from educational methods to punitive legal measures.[3]

> *Physicians' reluctance to discuss end-of-life decision making has been documented in other studies.*

In our experience, physicians are not always the initiators of these conversations. Nurses, patients, or family members are as likely to initiate these conversations as are physicians. In fact, if the fear of inciting physicians' anger or of jeopardizing their jobs could be removed, nurses may become a valuable resource in facilitating the communication between patients and physicians about end-of-life decisions. This expectation seems appropriate for several reasons. Nurses spend an enormous amount of time directly caring for patients, particularly in ICU settings. During this time, they have the opportunity to become very familiar with the patient's and family's opinions, needs, and values. While a good physician will also acquire this knowledge, the simple fact is that physicians spend less time in direct contact with hospitalized patients and their families than nurses do. In teaching hospitals where physicians frequently rotate on and off service, nurses offer a stable reference point for patients and their families. They may also have significantly more experience in supporting patients and their families through difficult decisions and the dying process than young physicians do. We advocate a strong collegial role between nurses and physicians with regard to end-of-life decision discussions with patients. While we believe physicians are ultimately responsible for leading discussions of these issues, nurses should be encouraged to facilitate and augment these discussions.

It is inappropriate to allow a patient to suffer unnecessarily.

Another key relationship that Reckling touches on is the patient-physician relationship, reminding us that decision making in this partnership is not equally shared. We were deeply concerned that patients' wishes were overridden in three cases. Although the details of the decision to override a patient's wishes were not provided, we think that there are rarely sufficient reasons to override a patient's wishes. A healthcare provider is not obligated to break the law or to violate accepted medical standards at the insistence of a patient or family members. However, we suspect that these cases did not involve these types of conflicts. In our experience, patients' wishes are overridden either because a family member voices opposition to the patient's wishes after the patient has become incompetent, or the physician is unwilling to abide by the patient's wishes because of his or her own professional or personal ethics. In the situation where conflict exists within the family, it has been our experience that constant, firm, compassionate redirection of the family members to consider not their wishes but the patient's wishes resolves many conflicts. This process may take days. When a physician is opposed to honoring a patient's reasonable wishes because of personal or professional ethics, the physician should receive collegial counseling and assistance in accepting the patient's wishes. If he or she is still unable to comply with the patient's wishes, the physician should transfer the care of the patient to a colleague who is able to abide by them. An ethics committee consultation may assist in resolving such conflict, and should always be obtained in situations where conflict exists or a patient's wishes are being overridden.

Pain control

Our final comments concern appropriate consideration of the pain experienced during resuscitation and pain control for patients for whom DNR orders have been written. The ways in which pain is handled is also a matter that may be determined by relationships. Reckling notes that three patients were thought by the nursing staff to be experiencing pain. It is inappropriate to allow a patient to suffer unnecessarily. However, "unnecessary pain" needs to be carefully considered. The SUPPORT Study includes several points worth noting.[4] First, family members consistently rated the amount of pain they thought that the patient experienced at slightly higher levels than the level of pain reported by the patient. Second, although 64 percent of the patients in the study reported that they would tolerate living in pain, 36 percent reported that they would rather die than live in pain. Finally, about 60 percent of the patients in the study reported that they wanted aggressive measures taken to prolong their lives when they were presented with hypothetical but realistic scenarios that involved a high likelihood of pain and a low likelihood of survival. One possible interpretation is that patients did not understand the terms used in the study to describe CPR, DNR orders, and the scenarios. Another possible explanation is that the patients fully understood the choices presented to them, but were willing to tolerate a potentially high level of pain in order to take the small chance that they might survive.

Resuscitation

It is interesting to note that pain and suffering are frequently mentioned as side effects of resuscitation that should be routinely discussed with patients as they make end-of-life decisions. Some researchers have suggested that surrogate decision makers consider pain to be the most important factor when they choose among treatment options.[5] However, we were unable to find any systematic attempt to quantify the level of pain and suffering experienced by persons undergoing resuscitation.[6] Upon further thought and review of the literature, several concerns developed. The likelihood one will survive resuscitation and survive to hospital discharge and have a reasonable quality of life is dependent on the cause of one's cardiac arrest, the presence of comorbid factors, and the degree of anoxic injury to the brain. It is unclear from reviewing the literature how many people who survive resuscitation and achieve an independent life experience pain, or what degree of pain they experience. It is reasonable to assume that some degree of pain is experienced, but this has to be considered relative to the great benefit of surviving and regaining an independent life. For those who do not survive to discharge, it is unclear how many ever regain consciousness after a resuscitation attempt. The literature suggests that most failed resuscitations occur because of failure to adequately resuscitate the brain. This results in either a persistent vegetative state or brain death, two conditions that, by definition, are associated with the presumed inability of the patient to experience pain and suffering. If full resuscitation is initiated, or if CPR is initiated in a patient who is already intubated, it is because the patient has lost spontaneous circulation and, therefore, consciousness. If resuscitation acutely fails, the patient never regains spontaneous circulation and consciousness. In theory, no pain would be experienced because the patient is unconscious. It is difficult to know how much pain and suffering a patient experiences when temporary restoration of blood pressure and pulse for several seconds or minutes occurs, followed by loss of these and subsequent lack of response to further resuscitation attempts. For those patients who do not immediately respond to resuscitation and die, or remain unconscious after resuscitation, it is hard to support arguments that severe pain was experienced directly because of the resuscitation attempt. It is unknown how much pain and suffering is experienced by those who survive resuscitation, regain a level of brain function that is better than a persistent vegetative state, but die later. This uncertainty should be conveyed to patients or their surrogates.

End-of-life decisions are important aspects of the care of patients.

It would appear that most of the pain that a patient experiences is during the phase of their illness leading up to a possible resuscitation attempt, not the resuscitation attempt itself. This pain should be aggressively treated. In cases where pain control may shorten a patient's life, we think that the patient's preferences should be elicited and followed. In cases where death is inevitable and the patient is unable to participate in discussion regarding pain control and possible shortened life, we believe that adequate pain control measures should always be used, and should take preeminent importance over length of life.

End-of-life decisions are important aspects of the care of patients. Whenever possible, patients' preferences should be directly elicited. Physicians should be primarily responsible for initiating and guiding these conversations. They should receive training in end-of-life decision-making skills that begins in medical school and continues throughout their careers. Nurses should take a more active role in facilitating these discussions when they know their patients desire them and the opportunity for discussion has not been created by the physician. Except in rare circumstances, the patient's wishes regarding end-of-life decisions supersede all other considerations and should be respected. Finally, the issue of resuscitation-related pain should not be used to coerce a DNR decision from a patient or family. When there is uncertainty about the amount of pain that may be experienced, this should be conveyed to the patient or his or her surrogate. In cases where adequate pain control may shorten the life of a patient, a patient's preferences should be elicited. In cases of terminal illness where the patient's preferences cannot be known, adequate pain control should always be given, even if biological life may be shortened.

Notes

1. SUPPORT Principal Investigators, "A Controlled Trial to Improve Care for Seriously Ill Hospitalized Patients," *Journal of the American Medical Association* 274, no. 20 (1995) 1591–98.

2. B.M. Reilly et al., "Can We Talk? Inpatient Discussions about Advance Directives in a Community Hospital," *Archives of Internal Medicine* 154 (1994): 2299–2308; R.S. Morrison, E.W. Morrison, and D.F. Glickman, "Physician Reluctance to Discuss Advance Directives," *Archives of Internal Medicine* 154 (1994): 2311–18.

3. "Dying Well in the Hospital: The Lessons of SUPPORT," *Hastings Center Report* Supp. (1995): S1–S36.

4. R.S. Phillips et al., "Choices of Seriously Ill Patients about Cardiopulmonary Resuscitation: Correlates and Outcomes," *American Journal of Medicine* 100 (1996): 128–37; S. Borste, Personal communication with the authors, 21 February 1997.

5. J. Hare, C. Pratt, and C. Nelson, "Agreement Between Patients and their Self-Selected Surrogates on Difficult Medical Decisions," *Archives of Internal Medicine* 152 (1992): 1049–54.

6. K.A. Ballew et al., "Predictors of Survival Following In-Hospital Cardiopulmonary Resuscitation," *Archives of Internal Medicine* 154 (1994): 2426–32; F.J. Landry, J.M. Parker, and Y.Y. Phillips, "Outcome of Cardiopulmonary Resuscitation in the Intensive Care Setting," *Archives of Internal Medicine* 152 (1992): 2305-08; R. Berger and M. Kelley, "Survival after In-Hospital Cardiopulmonary Arrest of Noncritically Ill Patients," *Chest* 106, no. 3 (1994): 872–79; L. Bialecki and R.S. Woodward, "Predicting Death after CPR," *Chest* 108, no. 4 (1995): 1009–1017; S.C. Warner and T.K. Sharma, "Outcome of Cardiopulmonary Resuscitation and Predictors of Resuscitation Status in an Urban Community Teaching Hospital," *Resuscitation* 27 (1994): 13–21; S. Yamashita et al., "Prognostic value of Electroencephalogram in Anoxic Encephalopathy after Cardiopulmonary Resuscitation: Relationship among Anoxic Period, EEG Grading and Outcome," *Internal Medicine* 34, no. 2 (1995): 71–76.

4

The Sanctity of Life Must Always Be Respected

Beverly LaHaye

Beverly LaHaye is the chairman and founder of the organization Concerned Women for America.

Since the 1973 Supreme Court ruling in *Roe vs. Wade*, which legalized abortion, America has been sliding down a moral slippery slope toward the acceptance of euthanasia as an ethical choice. Although painful circumstances often result from a terminal illness—including financial, physical, and emotional stress—these factors can never justify taking a life. Life is invaluable and must always be respected.

In 1973, the United States Supreme Court created a new "right" when it ruled that abortion was legal. Since then, America has slid down a moral slippery slope. Life has been reduced to a question of convenience. This so-called "right" has become almost untouchable. Legislators at the state and federal level are reluctant to put *any* restrictions on abortion. And American tax dollars are used regularly to fund abortion programs. Although abortion clinics conduct major surgery, the abortion industry remains the most unregulated business in the land. However, peaceful pro-life demonstrators have faced countless court charges and laws restricting when and where they can exercise their right to speak freely about abortion.

Life as a "choice"

Abortion is a national tragedy in America. Over *30 million* unborn children have died—and countless women have suffered emotional and physical anguish as a result. But the tragedy does not end there. When the Supreme Court justices decided that the life of the unborn could legally be terminated, they qualified every human's right to life.

Now America faces the question of whether to legalize assisted suicide and euthanasia. Based on the moral reasoning our government has used

Reprinted from Beverly LaHaye, "Consequences of a Slippery Slope," *Family Voice*, January 1997, by permission of the *Family Voice*.

before, if the right to life can be *qualified* in the case of the *pre-born,* it can be qualified for the *sick,* the *elderly,* and the *dying.*

Recently, the Supreme Court said it will review the cases of two lower-court rulings on the question of doctor-assisted suicide. Two circuit courts of appeal earlier ruled that states could not enforce laws against assisted suicide. Likening the decision of whether or not to have an abortion, one court wrote "the decision how and when to die is one of 'the most intimate and personal choices a person may make in a lifetime,' a choice 'central to personal dignity and autonomy.'" Once again, life has been made a "choice."

A crumbling foundation

The Clinton administration disagreed with the comparison, saying the court was wrong to equate "the right to die with the right to choose abortion." Instead, it urged the Supreme Court to consider the social, moral, and ethical dangers linked to doctor-assisted suicide. Then it listed a variety of scenarios that could prompt assisted suicides if euthanasia were legal: A health care system that undertreats patients to save costs; physicians who do not take time to evaluate a patient's pain or fear of their illness; family members who are exhausted financially and emotionally from a patient's long illness; mistaken diagnoses; or a patient's fear of becoming a "burden" to their family.

But the highest court in the U.S. has already qualified life as a "choice." And state and federal governments have repeatedly protected that "choice" for almost 24 years. In addition, President Bill Clinton has actively promoted abortion since he was first elected to the presidency in 1992. *Life has been devalued.* Now, while America is grappling with the issue of euthanasia, many Americans have discovered little moral reasoning to grab onto. America has fallen down a slippery slope—and found a crumbling foundation at the bottom.

Learning the hard way

As we have watched the Netherlands' experience with legalized euthanasia and assisted suicide, the results have been telling. Although that country set up strict guidelines to prevent abuse, many of those guidelines are regularly ignored. Now more requests for euthanasia come from families than from patients. And one study conducted in 1990 found that in one year doctors killed 2,300 patients who wanted to die, assisted in 400 suicides, and took the life of over 1,000 other patients *who did not even request to die.*

The reasons those patients and/or their families considered euthanasia or assisted suicide may have been due to burdensome health care costs, painful or terminal illnesses, or emotional distress—among others. Those situations can be extremely difficult. Likewise, dealing with illnesses, physical handicaps, stresses of old age, or watching a loved one suffer from any of these situations is not easy. Similarly, any pregnant woman facing an out-of-wedlock pregnancy, financial stress, or an abusive spouse is dealing with painful circumstances. But these are not reasons to take life, whether by abortion or euthanasia.

Life as a gift

Life cannot be dismissed because of painful or difficult circumstances. Life has been given to each of us as a precious gift. To begin qualifying who should live will ensure our own destruction. Euthanasia advocates claim that the *quality of life* is more important and that individuals should be allowed to "die with dignity." They are supported by polls in America that continue to show a majority of citizens *support* assisted suicide in the belief that anyone should be able to choose how they die. Assisted suicide and euthanasia may soon be legalized in the U.S. But with new "rights" such as these, we will continue to lose our national conscience.

One woman asked America's leading assisted-suicide activist, Dr. Jack Kevorkian, to help her die. She listed several ailments, including *chronic fatigue syndrome,* as her reasons for wanting to die. Dr. Kevorkian complied. Once her death was complete, however, it was discovered that the woman suffered from being *overweight* and from an *abusive husband*—not from any physical illness. There was nothing dignified or humane about that woman's death. Circumstances caused her to make that decision and society complied.

Sliding toward destruction

This tragic story, the Netherlands' experience with euthanasia, and our own history of legalized abortion show that life is trivialized when we qualify who should live. But I am afraid this is a lesson America has yet to learn. And so our slide down the slippery slope continues toward destruction.

5

Euthanasia Is Consistent with Christian Beliefs

John Shelby Spong

John Shelby Spong is bishop of the Episcopal Diocese of Newark, New Jersey. He is also president of the Churchman Associates.

Historically, euthanasia was rarely practiced or considered. Using relatively crude medical methods, society and, in particular, the medical field, found itself struggling to preserve life. Without the modern technologies that are commonly used today to substantially extend life, the terminally ill died quickly. In addition, Christians held strict views regarding the sanctity of life and believed that death was controlled only by God. However, this strict, traditional Christian perspective is no longer appropriate due to the advances of modern medicine. Today, many terminal patients languish in hospital rooms in a vegetative state, being kept alive only by life support systems. The sanctity of life is ultimately found not in the physical body but in the soul and its ability to knowingly respond to others and maintain a relationship with God. Christians need to reevaluate their positions and engage in the present debates on euthanasia.

What gives life its value? What gives life its meaning? If value and meaning are removed from life before life ceases to exist, is it then still life? Do potential value and potential meaning attach themselves to fetal life that is so embryonic as to be only potential, not actual? Who has the right to make decisions about life that is only potential? Is it the society? Is it the affected individuals or the bearer of that life? Does the sacredness ascribed by religious systems through the ages to human life reside in our biological processes? Is biological life itself sacred whether it be human or otherwise?

It is around these questions that debates swirl in this century on such ethical issues as euthanasia, assisted suicide, birth control, abortion, animal rights, the use of animal organs and parts in human attempts to combat diseases, vegetarianism and many environmental concerns. In most

Reprinted from John Shelby Spong, "In Defense of Assisted Suicide," *The Human Quest*, May/June 1996, by permission of *The Human Quest*.

of these debates the emotional content is high. The person operates on the basis of an unstated but assumed answer to these questions that is passionately held. Frequently that answer is so deeply related to the core of the person's being that it allows no opposition. So the result is argument, not dialogue, and heat, not light.

One of these issues is today coming before our society with increasing rapidity and it requires of the Christian Church a response. Is active, as well as passive, euthanasia an acceptable practice within the ethics of Christian people? To state it more boldly, is assisted suicide an ethical option for Christians and, if so, under what circumstances? At our Diocesan Convention these issues will be a major focus of debate.

The first thing that must be noted is that these issues are peculiarly modern ones. A century ago and, in most cases, even fifty years ago, these issues would hardly ever have arisen. Throughout western history, society in general, and the medical profession in particular, has been passionately dedicated to the preservation of life. The assumption commonly held was that life was sacred, that it bore the image of God and that its limits had been set by God. So deep was this conviction in the Judeo/Christian world, that murder was not only prohibited among members of the same tribe, but it was also surrounded by powerful disincentives.

In the biblical code, when murder occurred, blood retribution was the legal right and moral duty of the victim's nearest of kin. To escape immediate vengeance and to determine whether or not extenuating circumstances existed, cities of refuge were set up for those who accidentally killed a fellow Jew. In these centers the killer could find temporary sanctuary until the case could be decided and the verdict rendered by the society. If the murder was in fact accidental, then innocence and freedom was established. But if not, then guilt and the delivery of the killer to the family of the victim could be pronounced.

Is active, as well as passive, euthanasia an acceptable practice within the ethics of Christian people?

Of course the killing of an enemy was not covered by this prohibition. Thus the Hebrew scriptures had no conflict in proclaiming that the same God who said, "You shall not kill" as part of the Ten Commandments could also order Saul to slay every "man, woman, infant and suckling," among the Amalekites (I Sam. 15:3). Even suicide was rare indeed in this religious tradition, so deep was this sense of the sacredness of life.

But in that world surgery was limited to the sawing off of a limb. Antibiotics were unknown. Blood transfusions could not be given. Organ transplants were inconceivable. Intravenous feeding was unheard of. Finally, machines or medicines that could stimulate the heart and lungs could not be imagined. The time of death did seem to be in the hands of God. Human skill could do little to prolong it. So the idea grew and became deeply rooted in the psyche of the whole society that the sole task of medical science was to prolong life. That was a noble value then and it remains so today.

The realities of our world, however, have changed dramatically. That which was inconceivable, unimaginable and unheard of is now a part of our contemporary experience. We have extended the boundaries of life to where the values and definitions of yesterday collide with the technology and skill of today. That is why the debate on assisted suicide now looms before us and that is why this generation must question the conclusions of the past.

Let me pose the complexities of this issue by asking a series of questions. In what does the sanctify of life reside? Is life sacred when pain is intense and incurable? Is it a value to drug a patient into insensibility for pain while continuing to keep him or her alive biologically? At what point does the qualify of life outweigh the value found in the quantify of life? Is life's meaning found in the physical activities of the body or in the relationships that interact with the person whose physical body is alive? If those relationships can no longer exist, should the body be allowed to continue functioning? Who should make the life and death decisions in this world? Should that power be given to doctors? But doctors today are less and less involved with patients as medicine becomes more and more impersonal and complex.

We have extended the boundaries of life to where the values and definitions of yesterday collide with the technology and skill of today.

Since doctors still profit from hospital visits to their patients, we must recognize that there is a financial incentive to doctors to keep lingering patients alive. Should this decision be left to the family members? But there are cases in which family members have profited from the death of a relative. Family members have been known to kill a parent or a spouse when they had a vested interest in that person's demise. Should that decision then be left to chaplains, rabbis, pastors or priests? But the religious institutions today are too weak to carry such a responsibility, since perhaps half of the population of our nation is today not related to any religious institution. It might also need to be said that even members of this professional group of "God bearers" have not always been strangers to self-serving corruption. Can the decision be left to the individual involved? Certainly that person needs to be involved in that decision if at all possible, but can it be solely the decision of one person? Should extraordinary care for terminally ill persons be allowed to bankrupt families? Where is the point where such care becomes destructive to the economic well being of the remaining family members? Because this generation is now capable of certain procedures, is there some moral necessity to use those procedures?

Given the interdependence today of the health of the whole society through insurance rates, Medicare and Medicaid, extraordinary measures to prolong life universally applied would bankrupt the whole nation. Already this nation spends more than 80 cents of every health care dollar in the last year of the person's life. Should such life supports then be available only to those who can afford them? Would we then be equating the sacredness of life and the values that grow out of that concept with wealth?

If health care has to be rationed, as it increasingly is in the managed care contracts, on what basis are extraordinary procedures to be withheld?

The values of yesterday are colliding with the technological and medical expertise of today, rendering the conclusions of the past inoperative for the future. That is why questions abound and debate rages around the issues of life and death at both ends of life's spectrum. Even the word "murder" is being redefined in this debate. Is a doctor who performs an abortion a murderer? Is Dr. Jack Kevorkian a murderer? Should he be prosecuted for assisting people into death when hope for those persons had expired? Is it murder for a father who can no longer bear to see his child in intense pain or lingering malaise when all conscious function has been lost, to take matters into his own hands? Is it murder for a wife of long years to order no further food to be given to her dying husband in order to speed his death? Would it be different if she placed a plastic bag over his head? Would one be more moral than the other?

The lines are so vague, the decisions so awesome, the fear so great, the values of the past so compromised by the technology of today, that by not facing these issues consciously society will drift into decisions by default and a new uncritical consensus will become normative. The debate must be engaged and Christians must be part of it.

I, for one, am no longer willing to be silent on this issue. I, as a Christian, want to state publicly my present conclusions. After much internal wrestling, I can now say with conviction that I favor both active and passive euthanasia, and I also believe that assisted suicide should be legalized, but only under circumstances that would effectively preclude both self-interest and malevolence.

Perhaps a place to start would be to require by law that living wills be mandatory for all people. A second step might be to require every hospital and every community to have a bioethics committee, made up of the most respected leadership people available, to which a patient, family members, doctors or clergy persons could appeal for objective help in making these rending decisions.

> *Since doctors still profit from hospital visits to their patients, we must recognize that there is a financial incentive to doctors to keep lingering patients alive.*

My conclusions are based on the conviction that the sacredness of my life is not ultimately found in my biological extension. It is found rather in the touch, the smile and the love of those to whom I can knowingly respond. When that ability to respond disappears permanently, so, I believe, does the meaning and the value of my biological life. Even my hope of life beyond biological death is vested in a living relationship with the God who, my faith tradition teaches me, calls me by name. I believe that the image of God is formed in me by my ability to respond to that calling Deity. If that is so, then the image of God has moved beyond my mortal body when my ability to respond consciously to that Divine Presence disappears. So nothing sacred is compromised by assisting my death in those circumstances.

So into these issues Christian people must venture. It is a terrain fraught with fear and subject to demagoguery by the frightened religious right. That is why the mainline churches must consider these issues in the public arena where faith, knowledge, learning and tradition can blend to produce understanding. This diocese will begin this process at our convention.

6

Euthanasia Is Contrary to Christian Beliefs

James Thornton

James Thornton is a Roman Catholic priest. He has written articles for the New American, *a magazine published by the constitutionalist organization the John Birch Society.*

According to the teachings of most traditional Christian groups, noble and compassionate intentions can never justify an immoral act such as euthanasia. Proponents argue that the purpose of euthanasia is to ease suffering and pain. However, God created pain for a specific purpose. Pain reminds Christians of their dependence on God and it reconnects them with their spirituality. To end a life prematurely is to assume the role of God and ignore his teachings and plan. Euthanasia is wrong and is contrary to Christian beliefs regardless of circumstance or justification.

One of the symptoms of a society in the grips of moral crisis is a tendency to refer to reprehensible acts by soft-sounding euphemisms, by names that do not directly excite human qualms or agitate scruples and that evade precise reflection on the reality of certain situations. For example, in our modern lexicon, abortion is called "freedom of choice," sexual libertinage is dubbed "alternative lifestyles," and certain forms of genocide-in-slow-motion can be made to seem more acceptable under the name "family planning."

Such are the mental tricks and the "word magic" employed to quiet the normal functioning of our consciences. Sadly, they work on a great many people for long periods of time. Like certain narcotics, they dull the moral senses and can eventually blot out such feelings completely.

This being so, let us examine a concept that is very old, that disappeared from civilized life for almost two millennia, and that has now begun its return, lifting itself ever higher on the distant horizon, like a huge, menacing, black cloud. That concept is known as euthanasia.

The English word euthanasia is derived from the Greek and means, literally, "good death." According to its oldest meaning, it signifies merely

Reprinted from James Thornton, "Defying the Death Ethic," *The New American*, May 26, 1997, by permission of *The New American*.

the relatively painless, gentle passage of someone from this life to the next, without necessarily any human inference or intervention. Even in the Christian tradition, we sometimes hear the term "good death" used in the sense that the departed person died at peace with himself, with his family, and with God.

However, an alternative definition, more in accord with contemporary usages, generally suggests something quite different: It indicates the bringing about of the death of a human being, either by suicide or killing, ostensibly to prevent extreme physical pain or mental anguish. Euthanasia, according to the teaching of every traditional Christian group, is looked upon as suicide or murder, plain and simple, and, until recently, was universally condemned in all societies whose roots grew out of Christianity. This teaching holds that a supposedly worthy end, in this case the termination of pain and suffering, never, according to traditional moral norms, justifies immoral or unethical means.

With the rise of revolutionary ideologies in the late 18th century, Darwinistic philosophies in the following century, and the concomitant decline in fidelity to Christian teaching, especially among educated classes, changes in belief regarding the dignity and value of human life gradually came to be more widely accepted. The full significance of this change in outlook manifested itself sharply for the first time almost 60 years ago, in one of the most cultivated nations of Europe—Germany, the land of Bach, Schiller, Goethe, and Beethoven.

Early in September 1939, shortly after the opening shots of what would become the Second World War, Adolf Hitler held an important conference with key legal and medical officials of the Reich government. Hitler had decided that, in view of Germany's desperate need for hospital beds to accommodate war casualties, a euthanasia program must be undertaken. The incurably insane, those suffering advanced cases of senility, and others suffering similar conditions were to be painlessly killed, opening, in that manner, numerous hospital beds for the war wounded.

In response to Hitler's conference, the chief medical officer of Germany in that era, Dr. Leonardo Conti, immediately began a long series of discussions with legal, medical, and psychiatric experts to insure that whatever happened was done in accordance with law. Characteristically, Hitler quickly became impatient at Conti's delays and, finally, arbitrarily dictated a secret decree. That document authorized certain officials to begin at once to "grant those who are by all human standards incurably ill a merciful death." Census forms, seemingly for statistical purposes only, were circulated to doctors requiring that they list data on all persons with certain incurable mental and physical debilities. Secret panels of medical experts were then convened to decide who among the patients would live and who would die. Many thousands, over the next five years, were thus quietly slain. But there is more to the story.

The Church cries out

Sometime in the middle of 1941, Clemens August Count von Galen, the Roman Catholic Bishop of Münster, received confidential reports about what was happening. With great courage, in July of that year, the Bishop delivered a dramatic, stinging rebuke to the persons responsible for the euthanasia program, in an open pastoral letter. Some weeks later he initiated private criminal proceedings in the public courts against the parties responsible, who at that time were still unknown to him. This was required, he explained to his flock, by German law. Any German citizen who had knowledge of a gross violation of criminal law was bound by that law to report it, and, if necessary, to take action to bring it to a halt.

Hitler, embarrassed by these shocking disclosures, ordered a halt to the secret euthanasia operation, but the program continued until February 1945. After the war, medical doctors, and others who initiated and took part in this program, were prosecuted and tried before Allied military tribunals, and a number of the more prominent figures were hanged for their complicity in these crimes. Ordinary Americans, and other people of the civilized world, were deeply horrified in those years by the idea of any government sponsoring such ruthless, immoral policies.

The incurably insane, those suffering advanced cases of senility, and others suffering similar conditions were to be painlessly killed.

It is a profoundly revelatory fact that the wartime German government was forced to keep this terrible program a secret from the German public. Such were the sensibilities of the German people in those years that even a highly authoritarian regime—indeed a police state—dared not allow the public to become aware of what was happening. Its panic over the public disclosures by Bishop von Galen demonstrates that even the Hitler regime, though it exercised total control of the German press, radio, and all other forms of information dissemination, as well as the police and all public education, nonetheless felt constrained by potential outrage from an aroused public.

Americans, in contrast, do not live in a police state—at least not yet. They still pride themselves on their maintenance of a system of self-government, and on an open society with unfettered speech and independent communications. Americans also take justifiable pride in the value they have traditionally placed on human life. Life may be cheap in other places in the world, among other peoples and under other governmental systems, but innocent life has traditionally been held dear, and protected, in America.

That remained true until about 25 years ago and the Supreme Court's *Roe v. Wade* decision. Until that time, the sacredness of innocent human life was shielded by law, but more importantly, it was protected by the innate decency and high moral standards of the American people, by an ethos set squarely on the solid foundation of 2,000 years of Christian teaching.

Moral blindness

French historian Alexis de Tocqueville referred to these American attributes when he wrote the following words about the America he visited in the 19th century: "In the United States the sovereign authority is reli-

gious . . . there is no country in the world where the Christian religion re-
tains a greater influence over the souls of men than in America, and there
can be no greater proof of its usefulness and of its conformity to human
nature than that its influence is powerfully felt over the most enlightened
and free nation of the earth." So it was, and so it remained until liberal-
ism began to eat away at this wholesome influence.

Some Americans of the 1990s, it would seem, have lost moral direction to such an extent that not only are they not offended by an idea that
did offend and cause shame to Germans living under the Nazi regime in
the 1940s, but they unabashedly lend support to the idea, even in public
forums. Curiously, many of the justificatory pretexts and rationalizations
expressed so frankly today are essentially identical to those quietly or
clandestinely advanced in the Third Reich: that we have limited resources
that should be expended on the healthy and not the incurably ill; that
the incurably sick are a burden on their families and on society; that it is
merciful deliberately to end suffering by active intervention—murder in
other words; that innocent human life is not a gift from God, but a condition or state of being the fitness of which is to be judged by medical or
governmental authorities alone, according to strictly pragmatic criteria.

One thin barrier separating events of 60 years ago in Germany from
the trends of recent decades is the distinction between voluntary and involuntary euthanasia. Theoretically, the arguments advanced today aim
towards the legalization of voluntary euthanasia only—that is, to en-
couraging the notion that those who suffer physically should be allowed
to request assistance from others (usually medical doctors) in destroying
themselves. In contrast, the German decree dispensed death primarily to
persons incapable of making any such decisions about their condition or
of expressing their wishes at all. While we must admit that this is indeed
a distinction, it is a very tenuous one.

Eliminating "useless eaters"

British writer and philosopher G.K. Chesterton wrote decades ago that
the proponents of euthanasia always begin first by seeking the death of
those who are nuisances to themselves, but inevitably move on to the
next step, seeking death for those who are nuisances to others, once the
first step becomes customary. Let us remember that in a bloated, bureau-
cratic welfare state such as ours, where the government assumes a rapidly
expanding role in our lives, where the moral standards have fallen, and
where shrinking resources are stretched ever tighter to cover perpetually
expanding commitments, it is never long before government is forced to
make life and death decisions about "useless eaters" whose cost of care, in
dollars and cents, is quite high.

Anyone who surveys the expansion of government power over the
past 40 or 50 years cannot doubt that this is true. Whenever government
has stepped into some facet of our lives, assurances have poured forth
that we citizens need not be concerned, that no expansion of power is
contemplated, and that some benefit or largess will be granted free of
strings and without any obnoxious controls. Beneficence is always the il-
lusory motive, the grabbing of power and the promotion of evil always
the end products.

And of all power, the power over the life or death of innocents is the last one that should ever be willingly entrusted to government. Our own government usurped some of those powers with the Supreme Court decision on abortion nearly 25 years ago. Yet if liberals and other champions of big government have their way, that power will be vastly augmented not by the will of the people or of their elected representatives, but by means of another High Court decision.

Pain is an evil, without any question, but it is an evil permitted by God for a specific purpose.

On January 8, 1997, the Supreme Court of the United States heard oral arguments for and against the existence of a constitutionally guaranteed right of citizens to choose euthanasia, or physician-assisted suicide. This case, generated in part by years of media publicity about people suffering unbearable pain during terminal illnesses, points to the possibility of a landmark decision, one of those decisive turning points for the whole nation, as significant as the rulings about separation of church and state in the '40s, civil rights in the '50s and '60s, and abortion in the '70s. Like those baneful edicts of past years, this latest one, should it come to pass, will herald a dramatic new chapter in American history, one that further, and calamitously, devaluates life, and that opens new possibilities for government intrusion into the most intimate aspects of our lives. These possibilities frighten many people, most especially persons who are suffering various debilitating diseases and injuries and who, despite their difficulties, do not want to die.

Charles Odom, a 34-year-old resident of Mississippi and former Air Force officer, was injured in an automobile accident in 1984. He remained in a coma for three months after the accident and to this day is severely disabled, requiring the use of a wheel chair to move about. Though his condition may seem daunting to less intrepid men, Odom remains fiercely independent of outside help. Charles Odom traveled all the way from his home to the nation's capital to demonstrate with other disabled people in front of the Supreme Court building. His blunt statement to the press about the Supreme Court deliberations is eloquent in its simplicity: "The worry is that if there's a right to assisted suicide, it will be used to get rid of us." It is easy to imagine bureaucrats and politicians scoffing at this fear, but a quick look at reality shows that it is by no means groundless.

"Without explicit request"

First, as we have seen, what Mr. Odom speaks of is precisely what has happened in other countries at other times. But we need not go back 60 years to Nazi Germany to find a chilling example. Current practices in the Netherlands are enough to give pause to any sensible man or woman. Years ago, the Netherlands changed its laws to permit euthanasia in certain circumstances. At first, physician-assisted suicide for people terminally ill was all that was allowed. Quickly, it was extended to the chronically ill, then to those with psychological afflictions, and finally to those unable to make such decisions at all. In the cold euphemism of the Dutch medical profession, the last category is known as "termination of the patient without explicit request" (suggesting dishonestly, perhaps, that the patient had somehow implicitly requested it). It is documented that each year Dutch doctors actively cause or hasten the deaths of 1,000 patients without the patients' requests. Guidelines and safeguards set down by the Dutch government to regulate euthanasia are routinely ignored, without serious repercussions to the perpetrators.

So, it seems, Charles Odom's fears are definitely not without foundation. In a secular society, driven exclusively by utilitarian considerations, to proceed from physician-assisted suicides to wholly involuntary killings of patients is a matter of inescapable logic, as soon as certain underlying premises are accepted—namely, that innocent life is not a gift from God and that government and medical authorities may do whatever they like for the "good of society."

We must now briefly consider the problem of people suffering long periods of extreme pain. That shibboleth is one that must be dealt with directly, for it is one of the chief weapons of the pro-euthanasia wing of the death lobby, just as minuscule numbers of pregnancies allegedly caused by rape and incest are the constant catchwords of the pro-abortion wing of that same group. As we have noted, much of the mass media has encouraged the present drift towards government-sanctioned killings of patients by medical doctors, through their sensationalistic exploitation of cases involving people with terminal illnesses who are suffering great pain. Does that mean, as the media assumes, that there is a close connection between pain and the wish to die?

Destroying a myth

According to Dr. Ezekiel J. Emanuel, associate professor of medicine and social medicine at Harvard University, writing in the January 7, 1997 issue of the *Wall Street Journal*, the connection between intense pain and euthanasia is a myth, fostered by pro-death pressure groups and the media. As a rule, Dr. Emanuel observes, it is rarely the patient in severe pain who seeks euthanasia. "Physical pain," writes Dr. Emanuel, "plays a very small role in motivating patients' interest in or requests for euthanasia." Most cancer patients suffering unremitting pain, for example, were more inclined to see euthanasia as unethical. Those more likely to seek or approve of physician-assisted suicide are rather those suffering from psychological factors, most especially extreme forms of depression.

The 1991 Remmelink Report, done in the Netherlands, where physician-assisted suicide is legal, disclosed that pain was the sole motivating factor in only five percent of euthanasia cases. Another study in the same country indicated that pain was the primary rationale in only 11 percent of euthanasia requests. Thus, the chief justification for legalizing euthanasia—that it is necessary to end needless pain and suffering—is really a lie. The vast majority of people in severe pain do not wish to die. They want life.

One cannot be oblivious to the reality of pain, or cold towards any human suffering. One cannot assuage pain with banalities, for pain is one of the most formidable facts of life in this world. From a medical standpoint, tremendous advances have been made in modern pain-relieving drugs and these help enormously. Various medical miracles mean that people rarely suffer pain to the extent that they did 100 years ago. From a spiritual, Christian standpoint, pain, though exceedingly unpleasant, nevertheless serves some definite purpose in this less-than-perfect world of ours.

Purpose in pain

The great Christian author C.S. Lewis reminds us that man is a fallen creature, rebellious and filled with self-will. God reminds us in many ways that we must be dependent on Him and must restrain the impulse to "go it alone." One of those ways is through pain. Pain is an evil, without any question, but it is an evil permitted by God for a specific purpose. "The human spirit will not even begin to try to surrender self-will as long as all seems to be well with it," Lewis comments. Many sorts of evil conceal themselves behind facades of contentment and pleasure. These, he says, represent "masked evil." But, pain "is unmasked, unmistakable evil." Lewis writes that "pain is not only immediately recognizable evil, but evil impossible to ignore. We can rest contentedly in our sins and in our stupidities . . . but pain insists upon being attended to. God whispers to us in our pleasures, speaks in our conscience, but shouts in our pains; it is His megaphone to rouse a deaf world." Man must be roused to the existence of evil, or else, as Lewis writes, "he is enclosed in an illusion." Pain demonstrates the existence of evil to an unmistakable degree, to a degree that no one can disregard. Pain tempers the rebellious human spirit, reminds us of our dependency on God and of our fragility, and turns us and our thoughts to the spiritual and the eternal.

That is part of a traditional Christian view of pain, and it is an incontestable truth that this view once buttressed the courage of our ancestors in the days before modern medicine, and helped them to gather the strength to cope with the considerable suffering and hardship around them. The only thing that can save our great nation today is for all of us to strive to emulate the steadfast faith and courage of our forebears.

Americans of these final years of the 20th century must soundly reject the twisted propaganda for death—that death can deliver them from pain and inconvenience. Doubtless, it is sometimes troublesome, and financially awkward, for some women to carry tiny children within themselves and to give them that greatest of all gifts that can be given—life. Sadly, some of them therefore shrug their obligation and choose death for their offspring, and millions of helpless innocents die. Likewise, it is bothersome and burdensome for some families to care for elders, for the sick, and for the severely disabled, and soon, they too may choose death for their kin, if our courts and politicians are allowed further to infringe on powers that belong to God alone. Millions more will die.

Ill-conceived and diabolical schemes by elected officials, and unconscionable decisions by arrogant judges at all levels in the federal judiciary, promise to make commerce in death as commonplace as commerce in cabbages. If that should comes to pass, then our nation will have taken an irretrievable step on the road to moral catastrophe and its twin companion, political despotism. We must prevent our country from taking so fateful a step at all costs, and we must do so now.

7

Legalizing Physician-Assisted Suicide Would Lead to Abuse

Diane E. Meier

Diane E. Meier is an associate professor of geriatrics and director of the Palliative Care Initiative at the Mount Sinai School of Medicine.

The risk of abuse of physician-assisted suicide outweighs the benefits offered by the practice. It is true that many dying patients endure agonizing pain that still cannot be satisfactorily relieved by modern medicine. However, if doctors could legally assist the dying in taking their lives, even carefully tailored safeguards would be unable to prevent vulnerable patients from being coerced into choosing death. Family members and health insurers would be tempted to encourage and promote assisted suicide, hoping to avoid extended emotional anguish and tremendous financial costs. Rather than legalize assisted suicide, society should focus on minimizing pain and try to provide the dying with more comfort and compassion in their final days.

A recent survey, which I cowrote, found that doctors are often asked by their patients for help in dying, but seldom honor these requests.

Some years ago, I believed that doctor-assisted suicide should be legalized and that terminally ill people in great pain deserved more control over the circumstances of their death.

It is true that terminally ill patients sometimes find themselves in truly unbearable circumstances. But after caring for many patients myself, I now think that the risks of assisted suicide outweigh the benefits.

Proponents of doctor-assisted suicide say that strict regulations can reduce the chances of abuse and protect the most vulnerable from feeling coerced. But rules would be difficult, if not impossible, to enforce. For instance, Oregon, the only state to legalize assisted suicide, has guidelines that mandate the following:

• *A patient must be mentally alert.* It is the rare dying patient, particu-

Reprinted from Diane E. Meier, "A Change of Heart on Assisted Suicide," *The New York Times*, April 24, 1998, by permission of *The New York Times*. Copyright ©1998 by The New York Times.

larly if elderly, who remains consistently capable of rational deliberation about medical alternatives. Intermittent confusion, anxiety and depression are the rule rather than the exception, inevitably clouding judgment.

• *A patient must be within six months of death.* Abundant evidence shows that accurately predicting when patients are going to die doesn't become possible until just days before death. The guidelines assume that such a prognosis is possible and deny the uncertainty inherent in such predictions.

• *A doctor must certify that the patient's decision is not coerced.* This is an impossible task, given the financial and other burdens that seriously ill patients pose to their families. Indeed, legalizing assisted suicide is coercive in and of itself. Society would no longer promote the value of each life, and instead sanction an expedient death rather than continued care and support.

I now think that the risks of assisted suicide outweigh the benefits.

The push to legalize doctor-assisted suicide could not come at a worse time. Spiraling health costs and our aging population have led to radical changes in how care is financed, with doctors and hospitals rewarded for doing less for their patients. Seriously ill people need help easing their pain, time to talk to their doctor, answers to their questions and reasonable attempts to prolong their life when death is not imminent.

If this kind of care were available to every patient, it would certainly reduce, if not eliminate, the desire for a hastened death. But legalizing assisted suicide would become a cheap and easy way to avoid the costly and time-intensive care needed by the terminally ill. It could be seen as an appealing alternative when resources are stretched and family members and doctors are exhausted. The terminally ill patient could feel subtle and not-so-subtle pressure to opt for suicide. Our society should not be reduced to offering patients a choice between inadequate care and suicide.

The proposed guidelines for assisted suicide are well-meaning, but unrealistic and largely irrelevant to the reality faced by the dying. While I have had patients whose desire to die was compelling and understandable, such patients are few. The distress of the last days, when it occurs, can be effectively treated with analgesics and sedatives. Although we have the knowledge and tools to reduce suffering near the end of life, we are debating instead whether it should be legal for doctors to hasten death.

8

Ethical Arguments Against Physician-Assisted Suicide Are Misguided

Death with Dignity Education Center

The Death with Dignity Education Center is an organization whose mission is to promote a comprehensive, humane, responsive system of care for terminally ill patients. The well-known death with dignity advocate Timothy Quill is a member of the board of directors for the center.

Those opposed to physician-assisted suicide regularly cite certain misguided ethical arguments. Critics argue that legalized physician-assisted suicide would violate the Hippocratic Oath, erode the trust between doctors and patients, violate the sanctity of life, and start society down the "slippery slope" toward involuntary death. However, these concerns are based on outdated traditions and fail to take into account the impact of modern medicine and its ability to indefinitely defer death. The arguments also fail to acknowledge that laws and regulations that are strictly enforced can prevent abuse of the practice.

Opponents of physician-assisted death use several ethics based arguments that, in analysis, do not hold up.
• Misconception 1: Physician-assisted death violates the Hippocratic Oath.

This justly famous oath of ethical conduct, taken by physicians since at least the Middle Ages, has always been interpreted so as to relate to contemporary society and medical technique. When the suffering terminally ill patient begs for release from the grip of technology that Hippocrates never envisioned, his oath must be heeded in the way he intended—as dedicating the physician to serve always—and only—the patient's best interests.
• Misconception 2: The possibility of physician-assisted death would erode the doctor-patient relationship of trust and confidence.

The doctor-patient relationship has already been eroded seriously by

Reprinted, with permission, from the Death with Dignity Education Center's factsheet "Misconceptions in the Debate on Death with Dignity," January 1997.

many factors: excessive costs, unequal access to care, managed care, for-profit hospitals and so on. The relationship can only erode further when a patient cannot be certain that the physician will follow his or her wishes. Assisted death would not be at the physician's whim but would become available only when soberly requested by the capable patient as a release from unbearable suffering.

• Misconception 3: Physician-assisted death is a "slippery slope" that, if permitted, will lead inexorably to involuntary euthanasia—the killing of inconvenient, demented and other "undesirable" people.

The business of law is to draw lines in areas of social debate. It is legal to sell liquor, but not to children; it is legal to travel 65 miles per hour on some superhighways, but not downtown; addictive drugs may be sold, but only with a prescription. State regulation of physician-assisted death can and should provide strict guidelines and strict penalties for violators, as with any law.

• Misconception 4: Physician-assisted death allows patients to evade the need to face death as a fact of life, which is sacred and must be left in the hands of God or Nature.

Modern medical technology and health care have long since removed a great deal of death from the hands of God or Nature. Millions now live who once would have died routinely of birth trauma, infection, injury and disease. Physician-assisted death is an alternative to the end-stage terminal suffering that can and should be as obsolete as death from smallpox. A considered request for hastened death, far from an evasion of the situation, signifies the ultimate acceptance of it.

9

No Ethical Distinction Exists Between Active and Passive Euthanasia

Patrick D. Hopkins

Patrick D. Hopkins is an assistant professor of philosophy at Ripon College in Ripon, Wisconsin. He specializes in bioethics, social philosophy, and science and technology studies. He edited Sex/Machine: A Reader in Gender, Culture and Technology.

Many argue that an ethical distinction exists between the act of passive euthanasia (letting a patient die by withdrawing treatment) and active euthanasia (the act of killing a patient). However, the crux of their arguments usually rests on an irrelevant distinction between artificial and biological means of sustaining life. An artificial respirator and a human lung perform the same function of keeping a person alive. If a doctor removed a patient's lungs, causing the patient's death, that doctor would be killing. Similarly, if a doctor removed a respirator from a patient, causing death, that doctor would be killing. Functionally and ethically speaking, both cases are indistinct. Therefore, passive and active euthanasia are both acts of mercy killing. Furthermore, if it is considered morally acceptable to withdraw treatment to end a life, then it should be equally acceptable to administer a lethal drug to a dying person who is found to be in a hopeless and painful situation.

At least since the publication of James Rachels' well-known paper, the distinction between passive and active euthanasia has been criticized for depending on problematic conceptions of causation and on the belief that the sheer difference between killing and letting die is morally relevant.[1] In fact, most of the debate on the passive/active and killing/letting die dichotomies has focused on conceptual issues of ordinary notions of causation or on the social utility of retaining those ordinary notions. But both the passive/active distinction and its clinical application depend on

Reprinted from Patrick D. Hopkins, "Why Does Removing Machines Count as "Passive" Euthanasia?" *Hastings Center Report*, May/June 1997, by permission of the author and the *Hastings Center Report*.

other assumptions that have so far largely escaped the notice of ethicists. In looking at which actions actually count as "passive" and which actually count as "active," it is clear that the practice of euthanasia consistently revolves around notions of a "natural" death, the "natural" course of disease, and the contextual permissibility of "unplugging machines" and "withdrawing treatments." Subtly but crucially evident in these concerns is a conceptual reliance on a form of the nature/culture distinction—the distinction between the "natural" and the "artificial"—and on particular assumptions about the definition and moral relevance of technology. As with the traditional issues of causation, there are serious conceptual problems in these assumptions.

Intervention and "natural" death

The effects of the nature/culture distinction and the concept of "naturalness" in the ethical discourse on euthanasia can be located by examining another common term in medical discourse—"intervention." Consider these instances:

> Death has always been inevitable, a "fact of life." But where humans were once helpless onlookers in the presence of death, we are now increasingly able to *intervene* in the process, using technological resources to direct or delay the inevitable.[2] (emphasis added)

> Consider, for example, the patient on a respirator with I.V. lines whose heart stops beating to the point that it cannot be started. Such a person is surely dead, yet we would not bury him with the respirator running and the I.V. lines in place. For aesthetic reasons we would first remove the *interventions* (p. 31). (emphasis added)

> . . . for physicians and medical scientists *intervene* in numerous ways in the lives of adult humans, children, infants, fetuses, and laboratory mice.[3] (emphasis added)

> . . . human medical *interventions* have interrupted the natural death process to such an extent that very few illnesses can be said to have a natural course.[4] (emphasis added)

> Title of prominent medical ethics textbook: "*Intervention and Reflection: Basic Issues in Medical Ethics.*"[5] (emphasis added)

What is the conceptual and moral effect of characterizing some action as an intervention? In euthanasia discourse, using this term separates out certain actions and objects as ontologically distinct, giving those actions and objects a special status in relation to surrounding phenomena. If a respirator, for example, is considered an intervention, then it is somehow ontologically isolated—inserted, foreign, added-on—from that in which it intervenes. More importantly, however, is what intervention implies about the larger phenomena in which it occurs.

It makes sense to call something an intervention only if one perceives that the collection of phenomena before the intervention forms an identifiable process. In fact, calling something an intervention may be the constructive act by which pre-intervention phenomena come to be related (as calling something pathological often establishes what will be considered normal). These phenomena are viewed as being gathered together to form a socially and morally meaningful, addressable, coherent process. By labeling some action or object an intervention, speakers impute an ontological and moral character to the pre-intervention phenomena, giving them the veneer of continuous independent reality into which humans insert themselves. In talking of our interventions we simultaneously talk of those times, places, and events in which we are not intervening. This is an important discursive effect, separating out some phenomena as prior to medical action, indeed often describing them as if they were prior to human action in general. The discursive space thus created is centrally a moral space, for perceived as an area where humans are not acting, it is also therefore an area where human moral responsibility cannot obtain— the commanding intuition being that I cannot be held accountable for what happens in the course of a process *before* I intervene in it. It is therefore a powerful morally performative act when a speaker claims an intervention has occurred, for doing so begins to delineate areas where medical personnel are causally related to the patient and areas where they are not.

The performative act of categorizing a death as natural has legal and moral effect.

But if the act of calling something an intervention is morally consequential, does that imply anything for a post-intervention reality? It does. It is not necessarily the case that the process being discussed is broken up into three discrete units (pre-, inter-, post-). Instead, the process—the phenomenon of a disease for instance—can be thought of as having a relatively continuous trajectory that medical intervention has interrupted. But, like a video paused when a doorbell interrupts or the concentration on a game which a passerby interrupts, one can return to the original trajectory of the process when the interruption ceases, or is removed.

Here is where the concept of the natural comes into play. For the term is often invoked to describe the character of the process in which medical action intervenes, or more precisely, to characterize the state and trajectory of that process once the intervention has been removed. Although the terms *natural* and *nature* have many shifting and selectively applied meanings, they often simply suggest "that which is not made by humans." When interventions are removed and bodies and physiological processes are returned to their natural courses, then, such language implies the withdrawal of human action, effect, and responsibility. Here let me recall some common and simplistic, but very telling, appeals to nature:[6]

> Passive euthanasia is allowing nature to takes its course.

> Passive euthanasia just lets a disease take its natural course.

> Active euthanasia is doing harm unto others, while passive euthanasia is allowing nature to run its course.

> I believe that passive euthanasia is permissible because it simply allows the natural processes of life and death to take their courses. Active euthanasia, however, ends life before death naturally comes.

The rough and ready implication of 'natural' in these comments is a moral one—humans are not culpable for that which they do not do. Therefore, any process that is modified by 'natural' in this sense is a process that humans have not caused, are not culpable for, and whose intervention in must be interpreted with regard to these ontological "facts."

When we in this way conceive of medicine as intervention, how does the appeal to naturalness actually shape the moral analysis of causation and responsibility—the key worries in the medical engagement with euthanasia?

"Natural" states as morally neutral

Recourse to concepts of nature, natural processes, and natural courses of disease in the previous comments tends to support the moral permissibility of passive euthanasia but not active euthanasia. None of the authors of these comments argued that passive euthanasia was somehow better for the patient or that active euthanasia would necessarily count as harmful. Euthanasia practices are not being divided up on the basis of balancing benefits and harms, nor even on complex notions of intrinsic or instrumental value. They are being divided up with an eye toward a kind of *moral and causative neutrality*. Passive euthanasia is morally permissible not so much because it is beneficial or right but rather because as a natural death, it is simply the kind of death that occurs when no one is there to cause death. This is what the language of nature, intervention, and natural processes allows people to believe, and paradoxically in many cases, to believe they can effect.[7]

The moral impact here is that euthanasia and the ethical character of a patient's death can be dealt with at a level of neutrality made possible precisely by these ways of speaking and thinking. One does not necessarily have to justify any positive act called "euthanasia" through the predictive complexities of a consequentialist ethics, nor through the tortured metaphysics of a deontological ethics. Instead, one can place the body in question into a neutral area of naturalness where its fate does not have to be justified as any particular decision, but simply happens, without the direct, discomforting involvement of medical personnel. The body, the disease, the death are not artifacts and thus the implications of human action and human culpability are deflected.

The assumed absence of human artifactuality and human culpability is apparent in the very category of natural death, in its juridical, ethical, and medical instantiations. For example, the goal of the medical examiner is to determine whether or not a death is natural. The performative act of categorizing a death as natural has legal and moral effect. Natural deaths are not killing and thus are neither illegal nor immoral, and do not confer responsibility.

The availability of a category of death with all the connotations of the natural opens up powerful and controversial possibilities. If deaths come in different ethical (and ontological?) sorts, then it is inevitable that the category to which particular deaths properly belong will be in dispute. The category of natural death, after all, offers protection, exoneration, and comfort. It is very important, then, in terms of the practices and concepts of moral culpability, which deaths get called natural and under what conditions.

The category of natural death, after all, offers protection, exoneration, and comfort.

Naturalness often attaches to certain deaths in the common medico-ethical distinction between killing and letting die. Implicated in the characterization of medical practice as intervention, it is typically thought that in killing a person one is the direct causal agent of death, while in letting die one simply allows an underlying physiological process to follow its natural course. This notion of causation has a complicated history, with suspicions about its philosophical and empirical coherence going back at least to Hume.[8] Its complications do not mean that it is ever really contested in practice; though its practices can be complicated. Baruch Brody writes:

> X has a right not to be killed against everyone since everyone has an obligation to X not to deprive X of X's life (where that means not to cause the loss of X's life). Notice that on this analysis the crucial point is that one violates X's right not to be killed when one causes the death of X. Causality is a very difficult concept. A tremendous legal and philosophical literature has been devoted to developing a theory of causality; despite these many attempts, no satisfactory theory has emerged. Some . . . have concluded that causality is not a concept that we can fruitfully use in making decisions. . . . This skepticism about causality is understandable in light of the failure until now to articulate a satisfactory theory of causality. It must nevertheless be rejected; causality is too crucial a notion for every aspect of the theory of rights. . . . If we are to appeal to rights in deciding which actions are morally permissible, we must presuppose that we can make causal judgments even if we have no adequately articulated theory of causality.[9]

My interest here is not in arguing any one theory of causality over another, nor in claiming that the concept of causality is unnecessary, or useless, or indefensible. What I want to point out is that in this passage (and many other philosophical discussions) causality is insisted upon not because it has been proven or even well articulated, but because it is needed to achieve some socially sanctioned goal—in this case making moral decisions and determining responsibility. Brody has us rely on a notion of causation not because of its theoretical adequacy but because of its moral necessity. And, of course, "moral" here does not mean that causation is somehow itself a moral requirement of a particular ethical system. Moral necessity here is a pragmatic requirement, essential if categories of moral discourse are to be effectual in social contexts.

Being nonobjective and socially embedded from the start, the assignment of causality in death, and thus the assignment of responsibility, will be affected and constrained by the vagaries of our pre-existing cultural categories and by the inertia of our moral language itself. And here we return to the category of the natural. Implying an absence of human action and connoting a comforting place in the telos of a larger cycle, naturalness appears in killing/letting die assignments as a moral-by-default, liberating goal. If medical personnel, government, family, friends, and patients themselves can only get to that natural state that results in natural death, then all are freed from the possibility of having killed. They all have only let die—and in a rights-based ethical-legal system, no one's right not to be killed will have been violated.

Somehow machines are morally (ir)relevant for death in a way that other things are not.

As an example of recourse to the concept of natural death and the presumed absence of human causation in such, consider two medical cases Brody analyzes.

Mr. S is a sixty-two-year-old man, apparently mildly retarded, brought to the emergency room with problems of lethargy and slurred speech. A CAT scan showed that the left hemisphere of his brain was very edemous and had a large infarct. His condition worsened and he eventually went into a coma and was intubated. Physicians told the family that death was not imminent and they could probably eventually remove the tube. However, there was considerable brain damage and he might survive for a long time as a human "vegetable." Physicians asked the family if they wanted further respirator support in case this status was the best they could hope for.

Ms. T was in a motorcycle accident when she was twenty-five, sustaining severe head injuries. She has been totally comatose for three years, showing no higher brain functions. She is fed by tube, requires regular airway suctioning, and needs extensive antibiotic treatment as a result of serious and recurring infections. She will likely survive in this state for a long time, but can never reasonably be hoped to function again.

Brody writes:

> It is helpful to begin by reminding ourselves that no appeal to procedural or substantive rights is going to play a major role in the resolution of these cases. Withholding and withdrawing care from these patients (respirator support from Mr. S and antibiotics from Ms. T) would not be violating either their substantive right not to be killed or their substantive right not to be harmed, since, as I have already pointed out many times, doing so would simply mean letting the disease process take its natural course. (p. 168)

In Brody's analysis, even though death will occur, and it will occur only following the (in)action of the physician, patients are not being harmed, are not being killed. Their deaths result not from medical actions, but from natural causes. By removing the apparently medicalizing antibiotics and respirators (after a certain point) the physician is able to demedicalize the patient, to remove the patient from the nexus of medical causation and responsibility. Important, too, the patient's newly restored natural state also allows physicians and families to "de-moralize" manipulations of the human body and its death. Because it carries this implication of noncausal relationship, the mere withdrawal of interventions places the patient's death into morally neutral territory.

To aid in producing a natural death, then, confers a comforting Janus-faced moral character to merely "letting the disease take its natural course." On one side, we withdraw from patients and their deaths, placing them into morally neutral territory where no rights are violated, no culpability is formed, and all morally relevant causal influences are outside human direction. At the same time, however, we do not think of ourselves as completely and utterly withdrawn from patients and their deaths as if they had disappeared—the perceived telos of nature and its cycles of life and death allow us to think that we have participated in a larger process. While distant enough not to be killing, we are still, as one ethicist puts it, "co-operating with a patient's dying . . ."[10] Cooperating, but not causing.

Special treatment for the "artificial"

Yet tagging a phenomenon as natural is not only about releasing physicians and families to behave in ways that lead to patients' deaths while maintaining their own causal innocence. Naturalness not only permits, it also restricts. Permission to let die, practically understood as permission to withdraw, extends only to certain kinds of phenomena in the world, taxonomized in terms of their relationship to the natural.

Reconsider Brody's two cases. In both cases the decision has already been made that the patients' qualities of life are so poor death would be a preferable fate. Steps are allowed therefore toward increasing the chance that death will occur. But because of the paramount concern to avoid causation and responsibility, only some steps are allowed. Medical (in)actions are restricted to those perceived not to violate any rights and, most importantly, not to cause the death of the patient. In these cases, this allows only for the withdrawal or withholding of medical interventions—respirators and antibiotics. Other options, such as lethal injections of morphine, or other kinds of withdrawals such as the withdrawal of oxygen from the room, are not allowed. These options are interpreted as instances of killing.

But if natural deaths follow withdrawal, then what exactly is eligible to be withdrawn? And philosophically more fundamental, what is it about the thing withdrawn that makes its withdrawal morally permissible?

Machines can be withdrawn. Somehow machines are morally (ir)relevant for death in a way that other things are not. This thinking arises in Brody's cases more than once. Removing the respirator does not kill, does not violate rights, does not do much of anything morally speaking, except very importantly, signifies for the law, the medical community, and the family a return of the patient to a natural course, ending in a natural death.

But, for Brody, antibiotics may be withdrawn as well. Antibiotics do not figure as machines in everyday uses of the term. This may be an anemic use of our terms rather than some kind of meaningful metaphysical distinction, but even if antibiotics are not traditional machines, they do count as a kind of medical technology. Technology, then, a broader rubric than machines, seems to be eligible for withdrawal. But what is it about technologies that permits their withdrawal even when the death of a human being is likely to be the result? What specific ontological and/or moral character does technology have?

The Karen Quinlan case

Consider this passage from Tom Beauchamp about the famous Quinlan case in which Beauchamp argues against Rachels:

> Karen Quinlan was in a coma, and was on a *mechanical* respirator which *artificially* sustained her vital processes and which her parents wished to cease. At least some physicians believed there was irrefutable evidence that biological death was imminent and the coma irreversible. This case, under this description, closely conforms to the passive cases envisioned by the AMA. During an interview the father, Mr. Quinlan, asserted that he *did not wish to kill* his daughter, *but only to remove her from the machines* in order to see whether she would live or die a *natural death*.[11] (emphasis added)

In this description important information is provided about Karen Quinlan's condition—information that seems obviously relevant to any consideration of her status and her fate. She is in a coma, thought to be irreversible. She is respiring. Her heart is beating. Her vital processes are active.

But we are also provided with other information that, though perhaps not obvious, ends up being equally—if not more—important in considering Karen Quinlan's condition. For what stands out as morally salient for the actions being considered (given the prior determination of irreversible coma) is not the mere presence of respiration or other vital processes, but rather the specific character of the patient's respiration and other vital processes. Karen Quinlan's respiration is "mechanical." Her vital processes are "artificially" sustained.

The specification of Quinlan's breathing as artificial and mechanical allows for its differential treatment. While honestly and truthfully claiming that he does not wish to "kill" his daughter, for Mr. Quinlan the artificiality of his daughter's breathing implies that it is the *kind* of breathing that can be interrupted, even with the possibility that it will permanently cease. Seeing the machines surrounding his daughter as inessential, as artificial, Mr. Quinlan believes that by removing them, regardless of the physical results, he cannot be said to cause his daughter's death. Although his manipulation of her respiratory functions could irrevocably end her respiration, merely by eliminating the machines he does not kill her but only restores her natural state. The principle here is that a patient being artificially sustained is not being sustained in the *kind* of way that necessarily morally prohibits interrupting their physical processes, even if death may result.

Beauchamp's passage attests to the second major effect of the nature/culture distinction in euthanasia discourse, in its incarnation here as the nature/artifice distinction. The artificial may be eliminated, may be withdrawn, may be removed, without signifying any essential or constitutive act upon the body affected—given certain determinations about the irreversibility of the patient's condition. The retraction of the artificial functions not as a positive action in itself, but rather as a kind of negation of previous actions. It is as if artificiality is *defeasible*. That which is categorized as artificial may not only be removed, but its removal counts as the annulment of effect and responsibility, not as a new or secondary effect engendering new responsibilities.[12]

It is important, then, to recognize the complex and consequential moral fragility of the artificial, especially against the subtle pseudo-simplicity of the natural. Part of the reason that artificial respiration can be removed without fear of its causing anything is that the artificial figures historically as essentially inferior, tenuous, secondary, and a poor human imitation of a "true," "real," or superior natural phenomenon—an idea some attribute to residual ancient Greek thought.[13] As artificial, Karen Quinlan's respiration is a mechanical imitation of natural respiration and is therefore eminently a human construction, a human work. In addition to the general disvalue attached to the artificial as inferior, the artificial and the mechanical are quintessential signifiers of human intervention and human responsibility. Not only is it the case, then, that the artificial lends itself to being removed because it is thought to be ontologically insecure. The artificial is also the perceived limit of the human, medical involvement with the patient. By removing the artificial, physicians think to eliminate, or at least relevantly reduce, the degree to which the patient's condition is itself a human artifact.

In addition to the general disvalue attached to the artificial as inferior, the artificial and the mechanical are quintessential signifiers of human intervention and human responsibility.

In the artificial/natural distinction, then, the discourse on euthanasia has recourse to a powerful taxonomy, a potent rhetoric for categorizing different modes of existence, modes of functioning, modes of breathing and circulation. Applying the label artificial generates difference—a different status for the phenomenon it modifies, a different set of emotions attaching to it, and a different set of obligations concerning it. Identifying some part or process of the patient as artificial, therefore, has practical and moral effect. One of these effects directly concerns killing and letting die. Margaret Pabst Battin describes a certain fuzziness in this distinction:

It seems easy to identify the conceptual distinction between the two: killing involves intervening in ongoing physiological processes that would otherwise have been adequate to support life, whereas letting die involves not intervening to aid physiological processes that have become inadequate to support life. But there are a number of ambiguous cases: on the one hand, removing a respirator may seem to be letting the patient die, because his or her lung function has become inadequate to support life; on the other hand, it may seem to be killing, because removing the respirator intervenes in the physiological process of air exchange in the lungs . . .[14]

There is a way for this ambiguity to be resolved, however, by thinking of the patient on a respirator as an artificially sustained being. Once the patient's breathing is artificial, once his or her vital processes are artificially maintained, once his or her very existence is perceived as a novel phenomenon, then certain alterations of physiological processes become merely the removal of artificial interventions.[15]

And here we return to the first prominent effect of the nature/culture dichotomy: moral neutrality. If the machines/technologies/artifices are removed from Karen Quinlan, then she is open to a natural death. Think how different it would sound, how different it would be, if nothing about Quinlan's status figured as artificial or mechanical. If Karen Quinlan were in a coma, and was breathing, but the coma was irreversible and her father wanted to terminate her pulmonary functions to see if she would die, it would seem like killing. Being artificial changes everything.

My organs are machines

If this analysis is correct in elucidating the important ways the natural/artificial distinction constrains and shapes the ethical framework of euthanasia, then now the most important questions can be asked. Is the special defeasible status of artificial phenomena justified? Should removing artificial objects and treatments only count as passive acts? Is turning off a life-sustaining machine merely an act of omission?

The answer to all these questions is no. The problem with the connection between passive euthanasia (or "acts of omission") and machines is that the age-old distinction between nature and artifice obscures the actual functional relevance of particular machines to particular bodies. What is often ignored is the constitutive function the machine plays in the coherence of the actual person.

Consider this passage from Daniel Callahan, which sums up a common perspective:

[I]t confuses reality and moral judgment to see an omitted action as having the same causal status as one that directly kills. A lethal injection will kill both a healthy person and a sick person. A physician's omitted treatment will have no effect on a healthy person. Turn off the machine on me, a healthy person, and nothing will happen. It will only, in contrast, bring the life of a sick person to an end because of an underlying fatal disease.[16]

But in deciding that it is permissible to remove machines, of what real significance is it here that a person is sick? Simply being sick is not in and of itself a reason to let someone die (nor to kill them). The only reason illness becomes a relevant consideration is that it can reduce the quality of one's life to the point that it is not worth trying to preserve it. It is only at this point, when life is assessed as either meaningless or more harmful than good, that we consider "pulling the plug" or turning off the respirator.

The machine for the lung disease patient has become part of her pulmonary system.

But the problem in the respirator case is that the machine we are going to remove *is* the pulmonary system of the sick patient (or more precisely, is an integral part of that system). That machine breathes for the patient; it is a basic functional component of her pulmonary system, just like lungs are a basic functional component of the pulmonary system of a healthy person. It is of course true, as Callahan states, that turning off the machine on a healthy person does not kill him, but this completely glosses over the functional role that the machine plays in the bodies of particular persons. The machine for the healthy person is not part of her pulmonary system. The machine for the patient undergoing a kidney transplant is not part of his pulmonary system. The machine for the patient having a leg amputated is not part of his pulmonary system. But the machine for the lung disease patient has become part of her pulmonary system. Removing the machine eliminates the patient's ability to breathe.

Now, at this point supporters of the passive/active distinction would say that we do not cause death when we remove the respirator because it is only the underlying inability of the patient to breathe that causes death. But this claim is going to be irrelevant without invoking some arbitrary conceptual machinations. What constitutes the "underlying inability" of the patient to breathe is precisely the lack of a working pulmonary system—regardless of what causal factors led to this inability, this is what it means. The same thing would be true if we removed the lungs of a healthy person. It is still the underlying inability of the body to breathe that causes death, again constituted by the lack of a working pulmonary system. Could we say, then, that we do not cause death in this case, but rather that the death is caused by an underlying inability of the body to breathe? Such a claim would no doubt strike us as ridiculous, and the reason it would do so is that by removing the person's lungs we have disabled his pulmonary system. However, if this is true, then it should also strike us as ridiculous in any other case where it is claimed that after disabling someone's pulmonary system we are not responsible for his death because it is only the underlying inability of his body to breathe that really caused death.

If there seems to be a clear moral difference between the case of disrupting working natural respiration and the case of disrupting working artificial respiration, then this must rely on some detectable and relevant difference between the two pulmonary systems. However, the only difference between these pulmonary systems is that they are composed of different materials, and that some of these systems are made by human beings. But how could either of these two differences be relevant? What is significant about lungs is not what they are made of, but rather simply their functional role in the development and behavior of the human body. Whether made of synthetic polymers, metal, genetically engineered tissue, or genetically inherited tissue, lungs are significant for what they do—gas exchange—not for some essentialized composition. The same is true for hearts, livers, or any other organ. After all, why does a lung or a heart ever figure as valuable in the first place? Why does the failure of a heart or lung generate special concern? Is it because they are made of biological tissue? The loss of an appendix or tonsils hardly generates similar concern and these too are biological. Many people willingly pay enormous amounts of money to have fat and skin removed from their bodies for cosmetic reasons, with the mere fact of the biological constitution of these substances generating little hesitation. In fact, the reason hearts and lungs and livers and kidneys are valued and their malfunction met with great concern is not because of what they are made of, but because of what they do. They make it possible for the human body to continue functioning, to continue living.

Although appearing in a different metaethical context, this passage from Gilbert Harman makes a crucial and appropriate point:

> Consider, for example, what is involved in something's being a good thing of its kind, a good knife, a good watch, or a good heart. Associated with these kinds of things are certain functions. A knife is something that is used for cutting; a watch is used to keep time; *a heart is that organ which pumps the blood*. Furthermore, something is a good thing of the relevant kind to the extent that it adequately fulfills its proper function. A good knife cuts well; a good watch keeps accurate time; a good heart pumps blood at the right pressure without faltering. . . . Then, for these cases, a good [thing] is a [thing] that adequately fulfills its function. . . . A knife ought to be sharp, so that it will cut well. There is something wrong with a heart that fails to pump blood without faltering.
>
> There are, of course, two somewhat different cases here, artifacts, such as watches and knives, and parts of natural systems, such as hearts. The functions of artifacts are determined by their makers and users. The functions of parts of natural systems are determined by their roles in sustaining those systems. In either case, though, it is a factual question what the relevant function of a [thing] is.[17] (emphasis added)

While still feeling the need to distinguish between artificial objects and natural objects, Harman nonetheless points out the functionalist realization. What makes a thing a good thing of its kind is how well it functions for some particular end. What makes a knife a good knife is not whether is it made of steel, bone, plastic, or glass, nor, I would argue, whether it is made in a factory or just found (as a sliver of rock). What makes a good knife is its ability to cut well. Even more strongly, but consistently, one can see that what makes something a knife at all is its use as a knife. The sharp sliver of rock is a knife if one uses it as such.

All the same is true for hearts (or lungs, or kidneys). What makes a good heart is that it circulates blood well. But the ability to circulate blood efficiently does not depend on being made of muscle tissue. It depends on the ability to contract and expand, to pump, to create changes in pressure, and so forth. What this means is that a heart can be made of anything as long as it can perform the function we consider to be the factually relevant function of hearts—and in fact this function is what makes something a "heart." Irrespective of its genesis, developmental history, or molecular structure, any object that performs the same function as a heart, lung, or liver actually is a heart, lung, or liver. "Artificial" hearts are hearts. "Artificial" lungs are lungs. "Artificial" respiratory systems are just respiratory systems.

In the moral debate about turning off machines, therefore, what is physically, factually, and morally relevant is not anything about being sick per se. It is about what constitutes a person's pulmonary system (or other system). For some individuals, it includes a physical system made of tubes and compression units nominally referred to as a "respirator." For some people, it is only a physical system made of tubes and compression units nominally referred to as "lungs."

The upshot is that when we terminate the function of a person's pulmonary system, we have thereby caused her inability to exchange necessary gases. In doing so, we kill her. Whether labeled artificial or natural it is our disruption of her pulmonary system that prevents her from getting air.

What makes a thing a good thing of its kind is how well it functions for some particular end.

While initial intuitions about causation, nonresponsibility, and removing machines may have agreed with Callahan, the important thing to see is that what counts as omitting treatment and acting passively in the first place directly depends on assumptions about the ontology, significance, and defeasibility of technology. Only if one assumes that there is a metaphysical, essential, and intrinsic moral difference between machines and natural bodily organs can one claim that turning off a machine is merely an omission, merely a passive act.

Of course, given the pervasive influence and long-term cultural inertia of the nature/artifice distinction, and the unwarranted metaphysical and moral prejudice against artificial objects and phenomena, there is no doubt that this functionalist account of respiration (or any other bodily process) and its consequences will still seem counterintuitive to many. However, I think that in many cases (though inconsistently) people actually do recognize the irrelevance of perceived artificiality, and do so for functionalist reasons.

For example, if I were to blow out the computer chip in a person's pacemaker with an electromagnetic pulse and the person died, it would seem to most people that I have killed. I know of no one who would take seriously the claim that the death was natural, because it was not I who caused the death, but rather the underlying heart disease. I sincerely doubt any court would take such a claim seriously either.

When we terminate the function of a person's pulmonary system, we have thereby caused her inability to exchange necessary gases.

For one, our culturally constructed notions of sickness and health get fuzzy here. Even though the pacemaker murder victim in some sense had an illness, which lead to a cardiac malfunction, there is no more malfunction as long as the pacemaker works. It is no longer a given that this person is sick, provided other debilitating side effects are not produced. The patient no longer has a cardiac defect. In this case, we would probably say, and would be correct in so doing, that this person is healthy—healthy because his circulatory system functions well. Regardless of whether his well-functioning circulatory system is composed of all muscle and nerve tissue, or is part muscle tissue and part silicon and plastic, its function is the physically and morally relevant consideration. The crime that would have been committed had I destroyed the pacemaker would be that I destroyed part of the circulatory system necessary for survival, killing a healthy, fully functional person. The artificiality of the system would retain little rhetorical appeal, little moral weight.

Perhaps part of the problem here is not a purely philosophical one, nor a medical one, nor quite a physical one. The problem is visual, practical, cultural, almost aesthetic. Contemporary respirators are not very efficient. They are too bulky, cannot easily be carried around, and require too much attention. Even if artificial pulmonary systems may be superior to a hidden set of rotting, pustulated, malodorous lungs, artificial pulmonary systems still look monstrous and given the inertia of our cultural categories, they can appear terribly incongruous inserted in and juxtaposed to our fleshy bodies. Their relatively primitive state and relatively unwieldy form lend themselves to the idea that by their removal, we only take away something extrinsic, inessential, something tenuous. By their removal we only return the body to its natural state, relieving it of the imposition of the chunky, noisy, metal box so the underlying illness can finish up its natural death. But would we feel so comfortable with such divisions and categories without the visual correlates of bulky respirators, or other similar devices? What if the respirator were small, clean, smooth, efficient, internal to the body, and did not interfere with quality living (but in fact permitted it)?[18] Imagine a respirator the size of an iron lung shrinking, getting progressively smaller, portable, efficient, invisible. At what point do we begin to get uncomfortable with the idea that simply turning it off counts as a passive action? What if this artificial pulmonary system ends up like the pacemaker or an artificial hip? If artificial lungs could be as efficient and as internal as a pacemaker, I suspect the notion that we could turn them off with causal and moral impunity would seem as odd as it really is.

Of course, one could say that the case of the pacemaker is different from the case of the terminally ill patient on a respirator, because the person with the pacemaker is living a life worth living—they are not dying, they are not in pain, they are nor comatose, in fact they are cured. This is *exactly* right. But what this points to is that our notions of natural death and the inferiority and defeasibility of the artificial only arise in moral rhetoric in these classic, pitiful, terminally ill cases. Something else is going on—something that has to do with the concept of futility.

I have been writing, in large part, as if artificiality and technology were always considered defeasible, but of course, as the pacemaker case shows, they are not. Other cases show this as well. Appeals to the moral permissibility of removing artificial phenomena only occur when a prior determination has been made that a patient is so poorly off it is thought better to die than to continue on living this way. Only when machines cannot do much in the way of improving a life, cannot restore a disintegrated personality, cannot achieve any curative end does technology become defeasible.

But although the appeal to the defeasibility of technology only comes up when we have decided death is a preferable fate, the technologies are not then actually any more special. Whether a patient's operative respiratory, circulatory, or other system is made of biological material or plastics, inherited or purchased, grown or manufactured, their operations are all equally futile if they fail to achieve some curative end, such as consciousness, mobility, freedom from pain, or the restoration of personality. Altering any of these operations is an equally active manipulation of the patient's bodily systems, of the patient's life.

Moralists are inconsistent in their claim that in turning off machines we only return patients to their natural states, resulting in deaths we did not cause and cannot be culpable for. It is just that in some particular cases, where we think the patient is better off unambiguously dead but are not willing to bear the moral taint of having killed, that the appeal to a natural death gives us a way out. It allows us to think that when we remove the machines necessary for living we are not killing.

The trap of "nature"

To a greater extent than one might have imagined, the nature/culture distinction, especially in its derivative forms as a nature/technology or nature/artifact distinction, provides a framework for the moral discourse of euthanasia. This framework is so much a part of our language, our ways of thinking, our ways of conceptually and politically dividing up the world that it takes effort to see how it constrains our ethical analyses and legal policies. But once explicated and subjected to scrutiny, the immediate conclusions are not complicated.

The straightforward philosophical conclusion following these functionalist arguments is to divest technology of its unwarranted specificity in moral discourse. In the case of euthanasia, this means recognizing that removing a machine is no different (functionally, morally, metaphysically) from removing a biological bodily organ if both systems are performing the same role. Both are cases of disrupting some bodily process. If this disruption leads to death, then both are cases of killing.

This recognition is not merely a move toward philosophical clarity. After all, if the mere conceptual problems of the terms *natural* and *artifi-*

cial and their applications were the only points against them, one could simply turn up one's intellectual nose at this aspect of euthanasia discourse and move on to other matters. Unfortunately, the rhetoric of the natural has serious effects, and while nature may be an efficient rhetoric for manipulating moral attitudes and legal culpability, it is not as efficient in preventing unnecessary suffering in patients' lives. Unnecessary suffering only seems to have weight when it is appealed to *against* technology, *against* artificiality, a common enough invocation in arguing to free patients from the "trap of technology." For example, Omar Mendez writes:

> Sometimes, because of legal issues, we are driven to the point of doing the inhumane by unnaturally prolonging suffering and pain when there is no hope for recovery, or artificially maintaining a body that has no cognitive functions despite the family's requests and even the previously expressed wishes of the patient.[19]

No doubt this situation is inhumane, in some generally agreed upon sense. It is harmful; it is useless; it is disrespectful; it is painful. However, the harm and futility do not lie in the fact that a body is being artificially maintained or unnaturally prolonged, but in the fact that the body is in a state of suffering and pain, or—if having lost all cognitive functions—a state of vegetative absence. Unfortunately, since so much of the moral passion involved in euthanasia rhetoric relies on the cultural prejudices against artificiality, bodies trapped in similar states not perceived as artificial are not allowed a similar escape. If a patient's bodily organs are biological and spontaneously functioning, then they are thought to be living naturally. Even if the patient is in pain, has no chance for recovery, or has lost cognitive functions, no appeal to unnecessary suffering, no appeal to our being inhumane will currently, legally permit us to free this person from the trap of nature.

If artificial lungs could be as efficient and as internal as a pacemaker, I suspect the notion that we could turn them off with causal and moral impunity would seem as odd as it really is.

But if we are cruel in refusing to let nature free patients from the trap of technology, we are both cruel and conceptually blind when we refuse to let technology free patients from the trap of nature. Fetishizing biological systems only prolongs a useless and horrible existence for those who are morally unlucky enough to have biological tissue, rather than metals, polymers, or plastics play the functional role of a renal system, circulatory system, or pulmonary system. When we remove machines playing these functional roles from hurting and hopeless patients, we kill those "trapped by technology." But this is not a bad thing. It is bad when we refuse to grant people trapped by nature the same benefit.

In this sense, much of the ethical discourse on euthanasia smacks of moral timidity. So I conclude this paper with a call for responsibility—not a call to take new responsibility, but a call to acknowledge that we are already responsible. Our moral practices already allow us to kill patients in hopeless and painful situations, as well they should.[20] It is a good kind of killing. But now we need to set aside our prejudices against the artificial and set aside our myths of the natural death and extend the option of good killing to those trapped by nature.

References

1. James Rachels, "Active and Passive Euthanasia," *NEJM* 292, no. 2 (1975): 78–80.

2. Robert Veatch, *Death, Dying, and the Biological Revolution: Our Last Quest for Responsibility* (New Haven: Yale University Press, 1989), p. 2.

3. H. Tristram Engelhardt, *The Foundations of Bioethics* (Oxford: Oxford University Press, 1986), p. 104.

4. Omar Mendez, "Death in America," *Critical Care Clinics* 9, no. 3 (1993): 613–26, at 613.

5. Ronald Munson, *Intervention and Reflection: Basic Issues in Medical Ethics* (Belmont, Calif: Wadsworth, 1992).

6. These kinds of comments arise with great regularity in popular euthanasia debates. These particular paradigmatic examples are taken from pre-med student comments, interview comments on television news, and personal conversations. These basic notions also arise in the bioethics literature, as becomes apparent later in this paper.

7. Margaret Pabst Battin, *The Least Worst Death: Essays in Bioethics on the End of Life* (Oxford: Oxford University Press, 1994), pp. 36–39.

8. David Hume, *An Enquiry Concerning Human Understanding,* ed. Antony Flew (La Salle, Ill.: Open Court, 1994). See especially Section IV.

9. Baruch Brody, *Life and Death Decision Making* (Oxford: Oxford University Press, 1988), p. 24.

10. Roni Simpson, "Nursing Ethics and Euthanasia," *Canadian Nurse,* December (1992): 36–38.

11. Tom Beauchamp, "A Reply to Rachels on Active and Passive Euthanasia," in *Ethical Issues in Death and Dying,* ed. Tom Beauchamp and Seymour Perlin (Englewood Cliffs, N.J.: Prentice-Hall, 1978), p. 249.

12. Beauchamp no longer accepts that we are never responsible for letting die, but he acknowledges that this position has powerful intuitive appeal and is widely held. See Beauchamp, "A Reply to Rachels," p. 251.

13. Paul Rabinow, "Artificiality and Enlightenment: From Sociobiology to Biosociality," in *Incorporations,* ed. Jonathan Crary and Sanford Kwinter (New York: Zone, 1992), p. 249.

14. Battin, *The Least Worst Death,* p. 16.

15. The cases of artificial nutrition and hydration are somewhat more complicated. Sometimes people do not even consider feeding/hydration tubes to be technologies. See Thomas A. Shannon and James J. Walter, "The PVS Patient and the Forgoing/Withdrawing of Medical Nutrition and Hydration," in *Bioethics,* 4th ed., ed. Thomas A. Shannon (Mahwah, N.J.: Paulist Press, 1993), p. 175.

16. Daniel Callahan, "When Self-Determination Runs Amok," *Hastings Center Report* 22, no. 2 (1992): 52–55.

17. Gilbert Harman, *The Nature of Morality* (Oxford: Oxford University Press, 1977). Relevant passages reprinted in *Ethical Theory*, ed. Louis P. Pojman (New York: Wadsworth, 1995), p. 483.

18. Work on creating such lungs goes on. See Stella Jones Fitzgibbons, "Making Artificial Organs Work," *Technology Review* (August/September 1994): 32–40. See Kemberly Ridley, "Artificial Sensations," *Technology Review* (October 1994): 11–13.

19. Omar Mendez, "Death in America," p. 614.

20. While I obviously take the position that active euthanasia is morally permissible, the issues addressed here do not generate any additional evidence for that claim, of course. This paper merely points out that removing machines is actually a form of active rather than passive euthanasia.

10

An Ethical Distinction Exists Between Active and Passive Euthanasia

Grant Gillett

Grant Gillett is an associate professor of medical ethics at the University of Otago in Dunedin, New Zealand. He teaches philosophy at Otago University and has published a number of articles and books on medical ethics. He is also an operating neurosurgeon.

There are many arguments that attempt to demonstrate that no ethical distinction exists between the act of letting a patient die, or passive euthanasia, and the act of killing a patient, or active euthanasia. However, these cogent and clearly premised arguments are usually based solely on ethical generalizations and theory and, therefore, fail to acknowledge the complex and subjective nature of individual reasoning and intuition about matters relating to death. Additionally, intuition suggests that an act of medical intervention that purposely hastens death clearly carries a different moral responsibility from an act of withdrawing treatment with the intention of allowing death to come about naturally. This is not to say that active euthanasia can never be morally acceptable. In some carefully considered cases, a doctor may be acting appropriately and responsibly by responding to the patient's need to die. But active euthanasia is ethically distinct from passive euthanasia and it should never be legalized or widely accepted.

> Any doctor, compelled by conscience to end a person's life, will do so prepared to face the closest scrutiny of this action that the law might wish to make.[1]

One of the authors of the BMA report on euthanasia argued that this statement should be followed by the remark: "It may be that the law, in its wisdom, will find that it cannot but agree with the moral judgment of the doctor concerned". However, it was not included.

I want to defend the conjunction of claims formed by these two state-

Reprinted from Grant Gillett, "Killing, Letting Die, and Moral Perception," *Bioethics*, vol. 8, no. 4 (1994), by permission of Basil Blackwell Ltd., Oxford, England.

ments; a conjunction which some find inconsistent and even hypocritical.[2] I will argue:

> (i) that killing a patient should remain against the law;

> (ii) that this action may, on occasion, be the only right thing to do.

I will also argue that it is generally right to withdraw life-prolonging therapy when certain conditions are met. Implicit within this position is the claim that there is a morally relevant difference between killing and letting die in the medical context of terminal care. I shall argue that this difference makes it wrong to legalize or accept active voluntary euthanasia as a matter of public policy, whereas the withdrawal of treatment can be justified and should be an open choice in certain circumstances.

    I. The "moral geography" of killing and letting die can be disposed around two orthogonal axes.

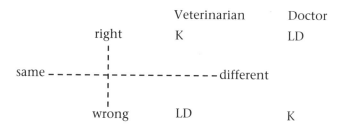

This scheme shows that if one believed that killing and letting die were the same, then one would have to choose whether both were right or both were wrong; but if one believed they were different, then one would have (a) to justify the difference in a range of relevant cases, and (b) to argue that one had correctly judged each as to whether it was right or wrong. The official medical position is that killing is different from letting die and that the former is wrong but the latter is sometimes permissible. This, as I have noted, differs from the stance of a veterinarian. The veterinarian's position is familiar and readily acceptable: it is sometimes right to kill an animal who is suffering or is bound to die in any event because that action spares the animal undue suffering. But can the doctor justify taking the opposite position just because the creature she is talking about is a human being? To do so, she must point to significant differences between killing and letting die in a range of human cases and argue for the moral judgments involved.

    In the animal case, the relevant considerations comprise pain and suffering as assessed from a "third person" point of view with respect to the sufferer. If the suffering seems too bad, no matter what opinion can (arguably) be ascribed to the animal, we euthanase the animal.[3] The first clue to there being a moral difference between the two cases is that we do not endorse such paternalism with human beings. The reason is that we generally reckon a person's opinions to be worth respecting in our moral reasoning. But this seems to strengthen the case for active voluntary euthanasia because we can ask the suffering person what she wants and, if she asks us to, we can, "help her to die". The importance of individual human choice, therefore, seems to tell against the unease about euthanasia expressed by those who take care of dying patients. But there is another possibility: the disanalogy between animal and human euthanasia may conceal submerged features of human death and dying that have ramifying implications for the problem in general and may be relevant to our conduct—killing or letting die—in terminal care cases.

In order to discuss the morality of active euthanasia, we must recall that actions are interventions in the world performed for reasons held by the agent. These reasons usually take account of morally relevant features of situations. Now, when an animal with a certain level of pain and disability is "put down", there is a more or less general specification of the situation which covers the moral features involved. We can, therefore, for the purpose of practical inferences, capture all the morally relevant aspects in a "mercy killing argument".

1. This creature's suffering is bad and unlikely to be outweighed by present or future pleasures or gains.
2. This suffering is unable to be stopped except by death.
3. There are no other morally relevant considerations besides the evident states of pain and pleasure or gain in deciding whether this life should end.
4. It is right to kill this creature to relieve its suffering.

But most doctors and nurses in palliative care practice believe that such a characterization falls far short of the understanding required in making judgments about serious illness and, in particular, about death and dying. They therefore contest premise 3 (call it "the completeness claim") in the mercy killing syllogism, so arguing that killing is different from letting die because of features inherent in the relevant range of cases. However, we must ask how we should regard their objections.

Often, in general clinical life, a clinician is presented with a problem which, as described, seems to be a puzzling diagnostic conundrum but, on interviewing and assessing the patient herself, readily identifies a familiar pattern. For instance, I was recently presented with a puzzling neuropsychiatric case description. I could not make a diagnosis until I had an opportunity to meet the patient, when it became clear that he was recovering from a primary diffuse head injury. This apparent shortfall in the describable or documentable features of a medical problem compared with actual participant observation is a well-known clinical phenomenon.[4] It is, in fact, a common feature of human cognition (and probably explained by the neural structure of human information processing[5]).

Aristotle argued that moral thought is most sensitive and acute in a particular situation when the moral judge has had relevant experience and training in such situations.

Aristotle argued that moral thought is most sensitive and acute in a particular situation when the moral judge has had relevant experience and training in such situations.[6] If he was right, this may be directly relevant to the moral assessment of a situation involving a euthanasia request. Elisabeth Kübler-Ross and Frances Dominica, both hospice workers, have observed that there are non-formalizable and particular (to the case) elements of any situation involving human death and dying which can and should guide our moral understanding. Frances Dominica remarks:

> Two things are clear to me. One is that mystery and a sense of awe surround death and whatever lies beyond it. The second is that an effect of love and grief exposed, the soul laid bare, is to bring forth reverence in the beholder. Here we find ourselves beyond the realm of reason crossing all barriers of different faiths.[7]

We might question whether it is reason in general or merely certain narrow conceptions of it that we have gone beyond here, but we can surely accept the central point. Kübler-Ross observes: "It is . . . not enough to listen only to the overt verbal communications of our patients"[8] and goes on to discuss a number of cases in which the message from the patient was not as it seemed to be. The subtleties suggested by both writers assume importance when we notice that the thoughts, feelings and attitudes of a person are pivotal in the moral aspects of a decision about human death and dying. For instance, some of our attitudes to suicide are related to the fact that we recognize the role of guilt, despair, loneliness and rejection in such actions.[9]

We should also note that the attitudes of individuals do not lose their force in relation to a life and death decision just because they cannot be defended by rational arguments.

We should also note that the attitudes of individuals do not lose their force in relation to a life and death decision just because they cannot be defended by rational arguments. Were a patient to say, "I know I have nothing to live for but I cannot bring myself to ask you to hasten my death", we would, of course, respect this thought. These "rationally indefensible" aspects of human value judgments may well express an intuitive appreciation which escapes more tractable (because less rich or subtle) descriptions.

Martha Nussbaum discusses just such moral perceptions in a study of Henry James's *The Ambassadors*. The novel concerns a sincere and upright person, Strether, who is sent to recover an allegedly errant son of New England from the dissolute life of Paris. He finds himself, as he gets to know his charge and the way Paris has affected him, developing perceptions and attitudes which tell against fulfilling his commission. The problem is that he cannot quite spell out, in simple and forthright terms, the morally relevant features of these considerations. Nussbaum speaks of the "moral significance of [a] . . . sense of life, for the vigilant and responsive imagination that cares for everyone in the situation and refuses the injunction . . . to simplify for the sake of purity and safety".[10] She is arguing against the moral decisiveness of clearcut reasons formed within a given conceptual framework. This is a deeply Aristotelian thesis in which Nussbaum tries to recognize the moral significance of the perceptions that become available to a character through participation in a situation. Strether finds himself unable to convey his perceptions to those working within a rigid New England code of ethics of which he himself has been sent as an ambassador. His own "reflective equilibrium" which, as Rawls suggests, is arrived at by a process of negotiation between his judgments and principles,[11] is therefore inaccessible to those for whom he is an ambassador.

The most common argument for euthanasia is that from respect for autonomy.

James confronts us with what Nussbaum calls "a morality of perception" which offers us the insight that reflective equilibrium on a moral issue in a context outside our normal experience must be based on an informed appreciation of the relevant perceptions. A "sense" that this is so might make those who know the situation impatient with demands for simple, denumerable premises forming "cogent, logical arguments" which are applicable to all cases of human dying, sufficient to sustain the completeness claim and taken by some to be definitive of the right answer to a moral problem.[12]

However, if the clearcut propositional reasons for and against are not definitive of what should be done for a dying patient, then formalized arguments about euthanasia decisions may be suspect. If, furthermore, the reflective equilibrium we reach on the issue should be sensitive to perceptions of this type, then we may need to reassess arguments which rest on a claim for the completeness of denumerable moral propositions.

II. The most common argument for euthanasia is that from respect for autonomy.[13] The familiar versions are neo-Kantian in form (but heavily tinged by liberal intuitions) such that, if one rationally chooses to die, that choice ought to be respected.[14] On this basis, one has a right to die as and when one chooses (provided, like all good liberals, one refrains from infringing any rights of others). Alternatively, a consequentialist could argue that a probabilistic and rational calculus of future goods and evils might persuade one that death was preferable to life and therefore also incline one to request euthanasia.[15] These views find practical expression in the Netherlands where a sane, settled and objectively reasonable desire for euthanasia expressed by a patient can be acted on by a doctor without fear of prosecution. These considerations suggest that societal endorsement of euthanasia is the morally correct choice. But the argument from moral perception casts doubt on the claim for the completeness of "cogent, logical reasons", thereby suggesting that the relevant moral choices are not always as clear as these models make them out to be.

First, it is quite unclear whether a dying patient rationally deliberates about her choices in any of the ways envisaged. It is, after all, unlike any other choice in that death is not, as far as any of us can tell, "an event in life: we do not live to experience death".[16] Thus, the situation essentially involves an unknown which rational formulations cannot easily accommodate. This forces the decision-maker into an, *ex hypothesi*, imponderable choice unlike anyone has made before; that choice is consequently made with neither the relevant practical wisdom nor clearly stable and adequate reasons for action. Indeed, people are not always sure, when they have opted for death and get a second chance, whether they would do the same again. From the evidence we have, it seems that some 98 % of people who do have the chance to reconsider a decision to end their own lives do not repeat that choice.[17] This suggests, perhaps, that the reality of one's own imminent death is not fully grasped until one has "stared it in the face". Having done so, one may not feel about it as one did in forming the intention to exit. Of course, in relation to patients with a terminal illness, this feature is less likely to be important as the patients have already faced the prospect of their own death. It also does not entail that we should discriminate between active euthanasia and letting die.

The retrospective ambivalence associated with suicide does not condemn us to nihilism about the worth of moral reasoning in considering euthanasia, but it does recommend a detailed, sensitive and attentive examination of human choices in difficult medical situations and of the particularities that may affect them.

However, a further justification for euthanasia, especially in the face of uncertainty, can be based on stoicism. A stoic lives according to the principle that one should control one's life by the exercise of reason.[18] Thus, if one finds oneself rendered incapable of the exercise of reason because one's life situation increasingly and distressingly resembles a smoke-filled room, then one ought to be able to choose one's own time to end that situation. One's mode and time of death ought to be determined by the same kinds of rational choice that guide one's life. But once again we see a reliance on an idea of reason and clarity of choice which are not typical of actual clinical situations where a kind of sensitivity and guidance is an integral part of good care.

From the evidence we have, it seems that some 98% of people who do have the chance to reconsider a decision to end their own lives do not repeat that choice.

Reasoning and sensitivity of the requisite type is central in Nussbaum's discussion of moral perception. She prompts us to ask "what role rules and universal principles can and should play" in moral decision-making.[19] She also asks "how the perception of particularity is connected with an openness to surprise, and how both are connected with a commitment to the cognitive guidance of feeling". And here we should notice, bearing in mind the nature of practical reasoning, Aristotle's claim that propositional knowledge of general principles falls a long way short of moral competence. The competent moral agent judges rightly in particular situations and successfully weighs the relevant general principles so as to arrive at perceptibly satisfactory moral conclusions. But this grasp of particularity, the "openness" mentioned by Nussbaum, and the idea of guidance by dispositions honed in practical experience, do not auger well for philosophical treatments of euthanasia because they call into question the adequacy of cogent logical arguments in moral judgment.

If these elusive aspects of moral reasoning are important in decision-making about euthanasia, we should worry about the fact that they are usually neglected in philosophical discussions (often based on simplified and under-described or imaginary cases). The need for a moral enquiry somewhat more attentive to what "in social and personal life count as something" is, we might note, a strong theme of Bernard Williams's recent thoughts on the nature of ethics.[20] But is this discussion relevant to the apparently clearcut distinction between killing and letting die? I have tried to suggest that the answer to that question depends to some extent on details of the situations in which the distinction is applied.[21]

A further justification for euthanasia, especially in the face of uncertainty, can be based on stoicism.

When a patient is killed by a doctor—or helped to die at a given time and place—the mode and moment of death depend on an irreversible choice made as a result of practical reasoning. This places a great weight on that reasoning and its adequacy to resolve the issues inherent in the human situation being addressed. It is not quite the same with the withdrawal of life prolonging treatment because our actions have a different dynamic. The description "appropriate treatment for the dying or terminally ill"[22] captures this dynamic and allows one to hold together the universal tragedy of death and the limitation of human action in the face of it.

When we intervene to alter a process which is at work in the patient's body, we intrude in what could be regarded as a *natural* change inherent in the form of a person.[23] Although defining what is natural is difficult, the increasing critique of the tendency to "medicalize" human life is good reason to take the idea a bit more seriously than a technology/choice based medical model would suggest. This critique has particular force in considering mortal clinical situations. A human being typically seeks active medical interventions so that she might enjoy continued life as a being with sufficient mental integrity to appreciate that life and this prospect justifies our intervention to override the bodily change. But a patient is far less sanguine about what she wants when she discerns that the process which has her in its grip is irreversible and may significantly alter her functioning as a whole individual. (Patients express this by saying "I have had enough" or "I don't want to fight it anymore" or "Is that really going to do me any good, Doctor?") Such responses can plausibly be taken as reflecting a sense of *the fittingness* or *naturalness* of certain bodily changes through which life is seen to be reaching a kind of culmination. At these points the patient tends to "listen to the wisdom of his body" rather than appealing to the unconstrained use of technology at the behest of so-called voluntary choice. (I shall return to this thought below.) For the moment we can see that such a feeling embodies what we might call "an awareness of substantial benefit" as the ultimate rationale of medical intervention. Such benefit relates to the whole person and not just a physiological process and takes account of the fact that we are all mortal beings. It can be cashed out as *a change that the patient now or in the future would regard as worthwhile.*[24] This may mean that the moral discussion of medical situations needs to find room for phrases like "allowing to die", "letting nature take its course" or "not prolonging the dying process". Such phrases are empathic with the phenomenology of the patient and are sensitive to the patient's perception of his situation rather than the medical challenge it poses. They call into question the unsupported assumption that in life and death situations we are autonomous agents with clearly formulated reasons for our actions and reactions and an unconstrained range of choices.

III. These empathic points about the psychology of the seriously ill or dying patient are highly relevant to a discussion of active euthanasia.

First, we have noted that the practical reasoning brought to bear on a decision to die here and now cannot have the rational clarity which philosophers call cogent logical arguments. The increasingly distressing "smoke-filled room" clouds our judgment as well as motivating our decisions. A patient may have pain which is often poorly controlled and is the focus of dire apprehensions. Here it is relevant that up to 98 % of patients who fail pain treatment in other institutions can be well controlled in an experienced hospice setting where pain as an affliction of the whole person is well understood and expertly handled.[25] Many of these patients will leave the hospice on lower doses of pain relief medication than those with which they were admitted, but with better control of their pain. Thus, it is perhaps not always pain *per se,* but the perceived significance of pain in terms of what it is doing and will do to oneself that may motivate certain euthanasia choices.[26] This is, of course, modifiable in ways that transform rather than merely make bearable the suffering that motivates demands for heavy doses of pain relief.

Second, there is evidence that a significant number (some would say all, but that seems implausible) of patients asking for active euthanasia are "testing" to see if others still want them around.[27] Some patients do feel worthless when they are severely debilitated and it is more than plausible that the external validation of their own self-attitudes may be of great importance to them. We know that this is a major factor in a number of suicide attempts and it would at least seem to be an open question whether it operates in euthanasia requests.[28] Of course, your question as to whether we still want you around receives a definite answer if I help you to die, but it is not clear that this is the answer we should give.

A seriously ill patient is . . . potentially subject to a number of subtle coercions.

Third, a seriously ill patient is also potentially subject to a number of subtle coercions. When you are admitted to a hospital for a procedure, you feel a definite obligation to go through with the course of treatment planned. Many patients will say something like "Well, I've come this far, I can't really back out now". It is an open question whether this reflects a genuine ambivalence or a rough and ready way of preventing indecision to reintrude once a decision has been reached. For most patients there are good, indeed compelling, reasons based on diagnosis and prognosis why the medical or surgical management planned should go ahead, but a decision about death is, as I have suggested, inherently less clear.

That lack of clearcut reasons is also found in the feared loss of dignity that apparently motivates some patients threatened with dementia or terminal disability. Most of us recognize that there are certain states in which we would rather not live and yet specifying this point is difficult. Indeed, it seems so difficult that to state when exactly the point of death should be is impossible. We normally deal with this by not striving officiously to keep alive and allowing a patient to die of one of the myriad ills that afflict very impaired individuals.

Most of us recognize that there are certain states in which we would rather not live and yet specifying this point is difficult.

The lack of clarity resides, in part, in a further feature of the reasons influencing our moral assessment of euthanasia. On the one hand, there are salient facts such as prognosis, pain, disability and so on which can assume the aspect of the only *real* features of the decision being made. On the other hand, there is an inchoate hesitation about choosing death which is supported mainly by ill-defined and poorly articulated feelings and perceptions. Although these contribute to an intuitive hesitancy, they are difficult to capture and lay out in the form of cogent, logical arguments. Faced with such "hard facts" and readily understandable arguments on the one side and merely a "fuzzy discomfort" on the other, those of us who support the traditional Hippocratic "respect for life" can feel somewhat weak in our protests. We have a real ethical challenge because almost everything that is easily captured in ethical formulations counts one way and almost nothing the other. But this imbalance depends on implicit norms which demand statable *reasons* for what we do and not just intuitions. I would like to suggest that this neglects the important and elusive moral weight that rests not on argument but on what "in social and personal life counts as something".[29] This directly recalls Nussbaum's discussion of Strether and implies that we can miss morally relevant aspects of human situations by not attending closely to our sometimes elusive perceptions and intuitions.

This is not to deny that medical ethics owes a great debt to the ordering and illuminating effect of principles like autonomy, beneficence and justice. These principles make sense of a host of messy examples and intuitive judgments that are otherwise hard to examine in an ethical way. But the very fact that we pause, wrestle and perhaps feel unsatisfied about the forceful arguments that demand our assent in this area means, I would suggest, that we have not got our minds around all that matters here.

We ought to be careful here that we do not exploit this moral indecision to defend a position which does not follow from it. We might, for instance, ask why the patient requesting euthanasia cannot "listen to the wisdom of his body" when he formulates his request. If he cannot adequately formulate his reasons, we have argued that he need not. Why, then, do we not allow his request to count as expressing the fact that his life has reached its culmination when he requests euthanasia? Why do we only accede to the patient's request when it concurs with the entrenched medical opinion which disfavours euthanasia but allows us to let a person die? Here one can always refine the case until one has eliminated all the myriad factors apart from the stark contrast between inaction and a lethal intervention, but I think it would be a mistake to do so. The possibility is that there is a holistic particularity to dying situations that does not admit piecemeal reduction to a series of factors, each of which can be shown to be morally irrelevant.

I have argued that there are a range of subtle differences in the particularities of situations which fall under the class of cases in which active euthanasia might be performed and those in which we accede to a request not to prolong life, and that these support what otherwise looks like a morally insignificant intuition that a life and death medical intervention (whether it prolongs or ends life) requires more justification than the acknowledgement that the appropriate response to a terminal illness is not to prolong life. This is part of a general recognition that we take a lot upon ourselves when we opt for death or life by medical means and that the actions of doctors and nurses are played out against a complex and difficult set of concerns which do not always admit decisive action.

IV. The first and most serious concern is about the technological bent in contemporary medicine.

Many see the willingness to kill, or even to allow to die, as somehow inimical to the practice of good medicine.

Doctors, particularly surgeons, are never more happy than when equipped with a powerful piece of interventional technology to serve as the definitive answer to a medical problem. It is clear that death and dying and terminal illness in general are "Gordian knots" of the first order for medical expertise. The patient is suffering, the doctor, *qua* scientific medical technologist, may be relatively impotent, and the problem will not go away. Intense personal factors are in play which are not obvious; often they are only obliquely expressed and demand a great deal of any caring physician. Something of the subtlety, depth and variety of these needs is gleaned from the writing of Elisabeth Kübler-Ross. She remarks (in a way that recalls Aristotle):

> To work with the dying patient requires a certain maturity which only comes from experience. We have to take a good hard look at our own attitude toward death and dying before we can sit quietly and without anxiety next to a terminally ill patient.[30]

In such situations, there are some doctors who shine; they engage their patients according to a *techne* or "artful skill" which involves, among other things, a personal and perspective grasp of how it is with the patient. Such a skill is developed through experience, incorporates practical wisdom and enables the doctor to respond to the patient in ways that give comfort, strength and even hope. This can form the basis for transforming what, in almost every way, is a tragedy. But it should be evident that in such a situation what counts as success is sometimes elusive and is not susceptible to measurement.

It is into this situation that we are tempted to march the *thanatologist/ telostrician* or whatever other name we might give him or her.[31] Like the surgeon who mentally has a knife poised to attack an appendix, drain an abscess or whip out a benign brain tumour, there is a definitive answer to this problem. This attitude is exemplified by one surgeon who remarked, "the only effective drug in medicine is iron, preferably in the form of cold steel". Not all surgeons and even fewer physicians evince such an attitude but, as a whole, we all become enthusiastic about clearcut interventional answers to medical problems. When there is an easy, instant and decisive answer to an inherently difficult and personally demanding situation, I believe that the conditions are ripe for that answer to gain ready acceptance. Euthanasia is just such an answer. Therefore, like any other medical technique that solves a persistent problem, its use may well do away with some of the finely balanced and participant moral judgment that would otherwise be required of us.

One of the facts that has led to major advances in terminal and palliative care is that no ready means has been devised to "magic away" the need for committed and thoughtful effort in this area. We cannot do away with the tragedy of death and dying the way we can an appendix or a meningioma; the "heal with steel" mentality will not do. It would be a pity if our moral uncertainties and reactions to death and dying were to be finessed in a hasty and ill-considered hijack of the area by clinical technicians whose thought focusses on means rather than ends. Medicine is more and more seeing itself as wielding a repertoire of definitive tests and procedures and, in consequence, its humane face is being effaced. I believe that euthanasia carries the potential to accentuate this change.

I should not like this to be thought merely a kind of Luddite argument fuelled by reactionary mystery-mongering. It is in fact predicated on the twin facts that we do not fully comprehend the human and moral dimensions of death and dying, and that there is an inherent unclarity and provisionality about many of the arguments that cluster in this area. One Dutch doctor with reservations about euthanasia remarked, "You don't know what you do when you kill a person. And it has nothing to do with medicine". It is this ignorance that should make us wary of a medical solution to a human problem.

The patient is often uncertain and even fearful about what their last illness might bring them.

The argument here is often cast in terms of brutalizing doctors and it is usually evaded by two appeals. I believe that both fail. The first appeal, based on the idea of specialist telostricians,[32] I have already discussed and found wanting. The second appeal is to the fact that veterinarians and doctors in Holland still care a great deal for their patients and do so just as much as doctors in countries where euthanasia is not practiced. There is a long and short answer to this argument.

The short answer is drawn from a comment by a doctor who has performed euthanasia in Delft, Holland: "I feel a bit Judas-like", "It goes against the grain".[33] I would respond: "How long will it do so?".

The long answer involves the *hexes* or habits of the heart of a moral agent. I have pursued this elsewhere and would only remark that the intent to kill changes a person in ways which are ultimately incalculable, even though they may be subtle and, for a deal of time, coexist with all the attitudes which provide checks and balances to any abuse.[34] Many see the willingness to kill, or even to allow to die, as somehow inimical to the practice of good medicine. I would not go so far, but would wonder whether the intuitions built up over the centuries of following *Primum non nocere* might be eroded were we to welcome into our collective psyche the intent to kill—albeit for beneficent reasons. We are, as Sartre noted, what we do and, in doing, make ourselves to be. Perhaps, as Philippa Foot has remarked, we need to keep up a substantial psychological barrier against medical killing.[35]

This last point has raised the issue of medical and nursing intuitions. What weight, if any, should we put on the common rejection of active euthanasia by health professionals. We return to moral perception; Nussbaum argues,

> if the ethical norm consists not in obeying certain antecedently established rules but in improvising resourcefully in response to the new perceived thing, then it is always going to remain unclear, in the case of any particular choice or vision, whether it is or is not correctly done. This does not mean that there are no criteria and anything goes. But it does mean that the standard will ultimately be nothing harder or clearer than the conformity of this choice or description to those of agents on whom we can rely for competent judgment . . . just as . . . the norm of good perception is the judgment of a certain type of person, the person of practical wisdom.[36]

If we concede that practical wisdom in dealing with a situation of a given type arises from experience of situations of that type, then we should look with special regard to those agents who are, all the time, immersed in the death and dying situation. These prominently include such people as Kübler-Ross, Dame Cecily Saunders and other leaders of the Hospice movement who widely regard euthanasia as a rather poor second best to good terminal and palliative care. Their intuitions have been arrived at with evident compassion for the dying and sensitivity to the moral conflicts involved, yet they tend to concur in rejecting euthanasia. Thus I would argue, as have Winch and Wiggins in other contexts, that such judgments are to be given special weight in the moral calculus in this area.[37] Therefore, even though medical intuitions are neither homogeneous nor decisive, there is a body of such intuitions which ought to be held in high regard in this debate and they tell against medical killing.

I would appeal to the same reasons to justify a moderation of the primacy of autonomy in a euthanasia decision. The patient is often uncertain and even fearful about what their last illness might bring. The patient may not see what might be done and perhaps sees no further than a painful measure of hours and days. Other things are, however, able to be found by those who, like Frances Dominica, are committed to finding them. The danger is that these elusive "goods" will be obscured and lost by the practice of despatching with the terminally ill.

If there is a kind of responsive perceptiveness in those who have many times worked through situations where euthanasia is an option, then their hesitations are of importance. We have seen that these feelings, impressions and reactions cannot easily be formalized with generality and may seem somewhat insubstantial when played against the confident and clear reasoning leading to moral approval for euthanasia. But I will again borrow from Nussbaum:

> We want to object that the feelings may after all in many cases be an invaluable guide to correct judgment; that general and universal formulations may be inadequate to the complexity of particular situations; that immersed particular judgments may have a moral value that reflective and general judgments, of whatever level of generality cannot capture . . . bewilderment and hesitation may actually be marks of fine attention.[38]

V. To some, the present discussion may have seemed obscure, evasive and elusive. I will make a more hard-headed point before I summarize it.

Many jurisdictions have responded to the wishes of patients to be allowed to die without intrusive medical treatment by adopting some kind of "natural death" legislation. And many have thereby "shot their patients in the foot"; "greater care must be taken to avoid the creation of a Kafkaesque legal nightmare for those we intend to assist".[39] Heintz, reflecting on the introduction of legislation into situations where clinicians and patients should be making mutual decisions about appropriate treatments, finds that it has hindered good care: "I am led to conclude that much of the well-intended legislation in the form of 'natural death acts' actually erodes patients' rights, jeopardises health care professionals and creates conditions that are sure to require litigation".[40] I fear a similar heavy handed effort to deal with active voluntary euthanasia.

The patient may not see what might be done and perhaps sees no further than a painful measure of hours and days.

I have suggested that our moral thinking in the area of killing and letting die should be "capable of doing full justice to everything that our sense of life wants to include".[41] However, our ethical discussions favour cogent logical arguments which can be relatively insensitive to uncharted human needs and values, and there may be subtle interactions between these and difficult life-choices. I have noted that clearly premised arguments tend to converge on the legalization of euthanasia and the moral irrelevance of the distinction between killing and letting die. Against this formidable ethical consensus, I have adduced some soft facts about the dynamics of human choice and the needs of dying patients, and an intuition about differential responsibility for our medical interventions over that which attends our acceptance of natural processes.

I have suggested that lack of clear knowledge of what it is to die, the possibility that the patient may well be asking questions about personal worth and role, and our persistent inability to identify cogent reasons to value human life despite its mixed gifts, all serve to undermine the ethical pre-eminence of practical reasoning in the face of death. I have also argued that the submergence of the human by the technical, the loss of responsive perspicuity and the intuitive discomfort of those most plausibly regarded as experts in this area tell against the condoning of medical killing.

These arguments do not undermine the principle that treatment can legitimately be refused by any patient and they allow physician and patient to heed "the wisdom of the body" in letting the patient die. I would therefore stand by my original conjunction of claims and echo Philippa Foot:

> Perhaps the furthest we should go is to encourage patients to make their own contracts with a doctor by making it known whether they wish him to prolong their life in the case of terminal illness or incapacity. . . . Legalising active euthanasia is, however, another matter.[42]

A doctor who intervenes to end her patient's life should do so knowing that the law disapproves of this act and that she might be called to close account for performing it. It may well be, however, that she has made the correct moral response to her patient's need and that any sensitive court of law would agree. In this, she and the law would show that type of mercy which may force us to desperate and unusual measures in tragic situations.

Notes

1. BMA, *Report on Euthanasia,* London: BMA, 1988, p. 69.

2. Dr Pieter Admiraal has accused me of this on New Zealand national television because of my holding the conjunction of claims I am trying to defend.

3. Other relevant considerations such as the costs involved or the existence of the requisite technology would not even be considered unless we had a certain set of moral views relating to the creatures involved.

4. M. Spitzer, "On Defining Delusions", *Comprehensive Psychiatry* 31.5, 1990, p. 386.

5. On this, see my "Representations and Cognitive Science", *Inquiry* (1989) 32: 261–76 and *Representation, Meaning and Thought,* Oxford: Clarendon Press, 1992 (esp. ch. 4).

6. *Nicomachean Ethics,* e.g. Bk II, Ch. 3 (for instance, tr. W.D. Ross, World's Classics). There is a helpful discussion in M. Burnyeat, "Aristotle: On Learning to be Good", in T. Honderich, ed. *Philosophy Through its Past,* Harmondsworth: Penguin, 1984.

7. F. Dominica, "Reflections on Death in Childhood", *British Medical Journal,* 1987, 294: 109.

8. E. Kübler-Ross, *On Death and Dying,* New York: Macmillan, 1970, p. 117.

9. D. Heyd and S. Bloch, "The Ethics of Suicide", in S. Bloch and P. Chodoff eds. *Psychiatric Ethics,* Oxford: Oxford University Press, 1981.

10. M. Nussbaum, "Perceptive Equilibrium: Literary Theory and Ethical Theory", *Logos* 8, 1987, pp. 55–84.

11. J. Rawls, *A Theory of Justice,* New York: Oxford University Press, 1980.

12. J. Rachels, "Euthanasia", in T. Regan, ed. *Matters of Life and Death,* New York: Random House, 1976, p. 39.

13. J. Glover, *Causing Death and Saving Lives,* Harmondsworth: Penguin, 1977, p. 184.

14. J. Rachels, *op. cit.* n 12, p. 43ff.

15. P. Singer, *Practical Ethics,* Cambridge: Cambridge University Press, 1979, p. 141ff.

16. L. Wittgenstein, *Tractatus Logico-Philosophicus,* tr. D. Pears and B. McGuiness, London: Routledge, 1921, 6.4311.

17. N. Kreitman, "Age and Parasuicide", *Psychological Medicine* 6, 1976, pp. 113–21.

18. T. Irwin, *Classical Thought,* New York: Oxford University Press, 1989, p. 173.

19. Nussbaum, 1987, p. 72.

20. B. Williams, *Ethics and the Limits of Philosophy,* London: Fontana, 1985.

21. This point was overlooked by Thornton in his otherwise very perceptive review of *Practical Medical Ethics,* in *Bioethics* 7.1, 1993, pp. 81–83.

22. B. Reichenbach, "Euthanasia and the Active-Passive Distinction", *Bioethics* 1, 1987, p. 72.

23. N. Poplawski and G. Gillett, "Ethics and Embryos", *Journal of Medical Ethics* 17, 1991, pp. 62–69.

24. A.V. Campbell, G. Gillett and D.G. Jones, *Practical Medical Ethics,* Auckland: Oxford University Press, 1992.

25. BMA, *op. cit.* p. 12.

26. G. Gillett, "The Neurophilosophy of Pain", *Philosophy* 66, 1991, pp. 191–206.

27. K. Gyllenskold, in J. Stanley and J. Mielke, eds. *A Casebook of Non-Treatment Decisions,* Lawrence University, 1986.

28. Heyd and Bloch, *op. cit.* n 9.

29. Williams, *op. cit.* p. 201.

30. Kübler-Ross, *op. cit.* p. 269.

31. R. Crisp, "A Good Death: Who Best to Bring It?", *Bioethics* 1.1, 1987 pp. 74–79.

32. *Ibid.* pp. 74–79

33. Personal communication to British Medical Association Working Party in 1987.

34. G. Gillett, "Euthanasia, Letting Die and the Pause", *Journal of Medical Ethics* 14, 1989, pp. 61–68.

35. P. Foot, *Virtues and Vices,* Oxford: Blackwell, 1978, p. 59.

36. Nussbaum, *op. cit.* p. 68.

37. I have argued this at length in "Informed Consent and Moral Integrity", *Journal of Medical Ethics* 15.3, 1989, pp. 117–23.

38. Nussbaum, *op. cit.* p. 69.

39. L. Heintz, "Legislative Hazard: Keeping Patients Living Against Their Wills", *Journal of Medical Ethics* 14, 1988, pp. 82–86.

40. *Ibid.* p. 86.

41. Nussbaum, *op. cit.* p. 73.

42. Foot, *op. cit.* pp. 58–59.

Organizations to Contact

The editors have compiled the following list of organizations concerned with the issues debated in this book. The descriptions are derived from materials provided by the organizations. All have publications or information available for interested readers. The list was compiled on the date of publication of the present volume; the information provided here may change. Be aware that many organizations take several weeks or longer to respond to inquiries, so allow as much time as possible.

American Foundation for Suicide Prevention (AFSP)
120 Wall St., 22nd Fl., New York, NY 10005
(888) 333-AFSP • (212) 363-3500 • fax: (212) 363-6237
website: http://www.afsp.org

The foundation supports scientific research on depression and suicide, educates the public and professionals on the recognition and treatment of depressed and suicidal individuals, and provides support programs for those coping with the loss of a loved one to suicide. It opposes the legalization of physician-assisted suicide. AFSP publishes a policy statement on physician-assisted suicide and the quarterly newsletter *Lifesavers*.

American Life League
PO Box 1350, Stafford, VA 22555
(540) 659-4171
e-mail: sysop@all.org • website: http://www.all.org

The league believes that human life is sacred. It works to educate Americans on the dangers of all forms of euthanasia and opposes legislative efforts that would legalize or increase its incidence. It publishes the bimonthly pro-life magazine *Celebrate Life;* videos; brochures, including "Euthanasia and You" and "Jack Kevorkian: Agent of Death"; and newsletters monitoring abortion- and euthanasia-related legal developments.

American Society of Law, Medicine, and Ethics (ASLME)
765 Commonwealth Ave., Suite 1634, Boston, MA 02215
(617) 262-4990 • fax: (617) 437-7596
e-mail: aslme@bu.edu • website: http://www.aslme.org

ASLME works to provide scholarship, debate, and critical thought to professionals concerned with legal, health care, policy, and ethical issues. It publishes the *Journal of Law, Medicine & Ethics* as well as a quarterly newsletter.

Choice in Dying
475 Riverside Dr., New York, NY 10115
(800) 989-WILL • (212) 870-2003 • fax: (212) 870-2040
e-mail: choice@echonyc.com • website: http://www.choices.org

Choice in Dying is dedicated to fostering communication about end-of-life decisions among the terminally ill, their loved ones, and health care professionals by providing public and professional education about the legal, ethical, and psychological consequences of assisted suicide and euthanasia. It publishes the quarterly newsletter *Choices* and the Question and Answer series, which includes the titles *You and Your Choices, Advance Directives, Advance Directives and End-of-Life Decisions,* and *Dying at Home.*

Compassion in Dying (CID)
6312 SW Capital Hwy., Suite 415, Portland, OR 97201
(503) 221-9556 • fax: (503) 228-9160
e-mail: info@compassionindying.org
website: http://www.compassionindying.org

CID believes that dying patients should receive information about all options at the end of life, including those that may hasten death. It provides information on intensive pain management, comfort or hospice care, and humane, effective aid in dying. CID advocates laws that would make assistance in dying legally available for terminally ill, mentally competent adults, and it publishes a newsletter detailing these efforts.

Death With Dignity National Center
520 S. El Camino Real, Suite 710k, San Mateo, CA 94402-1702
(650) DIGNITY (344-6489) • Fax: (650) 344-8100
e-mail: ddec@aol.com • website: http://www.deathwithdignity.org

The goal of the Death with Dignity National Center is to promote a comprehensive, humane, responsive system of care for terminally ill patients. It publishes a variety of information, including the pamphlet "Making Choices at the End of Life."

Dying with Dignity
55 Eglinton Ave. East, Suite 705, Toronto, ON M4P 1G8 CANADA
(800) 495-6156 • (416) 486-3998 • fax: (416) 489-9010
e-mail: dwdca@web.net • website: http://www.web.net/dwd

Dying with Dignity works to improve the quality of dying for all Canadians in accordance with their own wishes, values, and beliefs. It educates Canadians about their right to choose health care options at the end of life, provides counseling and advocacy services to those who request them, and builds public support for voluntary physician-assisted dying. Dying with Dignity publishes a newsletter and maintains an extensive library of euthanasia-related materials that students may borrow.

Euthanasia Research and Guidance Organization (ERGO)
24829 Norris Ln., Junction City, OR 97448-9559
(541) 998-1873
websites: http://www.finalexit.org • http://www.rights.org/~deatnet/ergo.html

ERGO provides information and research findings on physician-assisted dying to persons who are terminally or hopelessly ill and wish to end their suffering. Its members counsel dying patients and develop ethical, psychological, and legal guidelines to help them and their physicians make life-ending decisions. The organization's publications include *Deciding to Die: What You Should Consider* and *Assisting a Patient to Die: A Guide for Physicians.*

The Hemlock Society
PO Box 101810, Denver, CO 80250-1810
(800) 247-7421 • (303) 639-1202 • fax: (303) 639-1224
e-mail: hemlock@privatei.com • website: http://www.hemlock.org/hemlock

The society believes that terminally ill individuals have the right to commit suicide. The society publishes books on suicide, death, and dying, including *Final Exit*, a guide for those suffering with terminal illness and considering suicide. The society also publishes the newsletter *TimeLines*.

Human Life International (HLI)
4 Family Life Ln., Front Royal, VA 22630
(540) 635-7884 • fax: (540) 635-7363
e-mail: hli@hli.org • website: http://www.hli.org

HLI categorically rejects euthanasia and believes assisted suicide is morally unacceptable. It defends the rights of the unborn, the disabled, and those threatened by euthanasia, and it provides education, advocacy, and support services. HLI publishes the monthly newsletters *HLI Reports, HLI Update,* and *Deacons Circle*, as well as on-line articles on euthanasia.

International Anti-Euthanasia Task Force (IAETF)
PO Box 760, Steubenville, OH 43952
(740) 282-3810
e-mail: info@iaetf.org • website: http://www.iaetf.org

The task force opposes euthanasia, assisted suicide, and policies that threaten the lives of the medically vulnerable. IAETF publishes fact sheets and position papers on euthanasia-related topics in addition to the bimonthly newsletter *IAETF Update*. It analyzes the policies of and legislation concerning medical and social work organizations and files amicus curiae briefs in major "right-to-die" cases.

National Right to Life Committee (NRLC)
419 Seventh St. NW, Suite 500, Washington, DC 20004
(202) 626-8800
e-mail: nrlc@nrlc.org • website: http://www.nrlc.org

The committee is an activist group that opposes euthanasia and assisted suicide. NRLC publishes the monthly *NRL News* and the four-part position paper "Why We Shouldn't Legalize Assisting Suicide."

Bibliography

Books

Donald W. Cox — *Hemlock's Cup: The Struggle for Death with Dignity.* Buffalo, NY: Prometheus Books, 1993.

Ronald M. Dworkin — *Life's Dominion: An Argument About Abortion, Euthanasia, and Individual Freedom.* New York: Knopf, 1993.

H. Tristram Engelhardt et al. — *Euthanasia: The Moral Issues.* Buffalo, NY: Prometheus Books, 1989.

Samuel I. Greenberg — *Euthanasia and Assisted Suicide: Psychosocial Issues.* Springfield, IL: Charles C. Thomas, 1997.

Herbert Hendin — *Seduced by Death: Doctors, Patients, and the Dutch Cure.* New York: Norton, 1997.

Derek Humphry — *Final Exit: The Practicalities of Self-Deliverance and Assisted Suicide for the Dying.* New York: Dell, 1996.

Stephen Jamison — *Final Acts of Love: Families, Friends, and Assisted Dying.* New York: Putnam, 1995.

F.M. Kamm — *Morality, Morality Vol. II: Rights, Duties, and Status.* New York: Oxford, 1996.

John Keown, ed. — *Euthanasia Examined: Ethical, Clinical, and Legal Perspectives.* New York: Cambridge University Press, 1997.

John F. Kilner, Arlene B. Miller and Edmund D. Pellegrino — *Dignity and Dying: A Christian Appraisal.* Grand Rapids, MI: Eerdmans, 1996.

Rita Marker — *Deadly Compassion: The Death of Ann Humphry and the Truth About Euthanasia.* New York: William Morrow, 1993.

Robert I. Misbin — *Euthanasia: The Good of the Patient, the Good of Society.* Frederick, MD: University Publishing Group, 1992.

Jonathan D. Moreno, ed. — *Arguing Euthanasia: The Controversy over Mercy Killing, Assisted Suicide, and the "Right to Die."* New York: Simon & Schuster, 1995.

Starhawk and Macha NightMare, eds. — *The Pagan Book of Living and Dying: Practical Rituals, Prayers, Blessings, and Meditations on Crossing Over.* New York: HarperCollins, 1998.

Kenneth Overberg, ed. — *Euthanasia, Morality, and Public Policy.* Kansas City, MO: Sheed and Ward, 1993.

M. Scott Peck — *Denial of the Soul: Spiritual and Medical Perspectives on Euthanasia and Mortality.* New York: Harmony Books, 1997.

84   *At Issue*

Timothy E. Quill — *Death and Dignity: Making Choices and Taking Charge.* New York: W.W. Norton, 1993.

Periodicals

Tom L. Beauchamp — "Refusals of Treatment and Requests for Death," *Kennedy Institute of Ethics Journal,* December 1996. Available from the Johns Hopkins University Press, 2715 N. Charles St., Baltimore, MD 21218-4319.

J. Budziszewski — "Books, Arts, and Manners," *National Review,* July 14, 1997.

Cynthia B. Cohen — "Christian Perspectives on Assisted Suicide and Euthanasia: The Anglican Tradition," *Journal of Law, Medicine & Ethics,* 1996.

Commonweal — "Now the Hard Part," July 18, 1997.

E.J. Dionne Jr. — "No Right to Suicide," *Washington Post,* July 7, 1997. Available from 1150 15th St. NW, Washington, DC 20071.

Brian Eads — "A License to Kill," *Reader's Digest,* September 1997.

Jon Fuller — "Physician-Assisted Suicide: An Unnecessary Crisis," *America,* July 19, 1997.

Thomas Gates — "Euthanasia and Assisted Suicide: A Faith Perspective," *Friends Journal,* June 1998. Available from 1216 Arch St., 2A, Philadelphia, PA 19107-2835.

William A. Hensel — "My Living Will," *JAMA,* February 28, 1996. Available from the American Medical Association, PO Box 5201, Chicago, IL 60680-5201.

Nat Hentoff — "How to Commit a Loving Murder," *Village Voice,* February 17, 1998. Available from 36 Cooper Sq., New York, NY 10003.

Russell Hittinger — "Assisted Suicide: No and Yes, but Mainly Yes," *First Things,* March 1997. Available from Dept. FT, PO Box 3000, Denville, NJ 07834.

Lucy McIver — "Living Our Faith unto Death," *Friends Journal,* June 1998.

Diane E. Meier et al. — "A National Survey of Physician-Assisted Suicide and Euthanasia in the United States," *New England Journal of Medicine,* April 23, 1998. Available from 1440 Main St., Waltham, MA 02154-1600.

Sherwin B. Nuland — "How We Die Is Our Business," *New York Times,* January 13, 1997.

Caroline Balderston Parry — "About Choice and Suicide and Susan," *Friends Journal,* June 1998.

Larry Reibstein — "Matters of Life and Death," *Newsweek,* July 7, 1997.

Wesley J. Smith — "Death Wars," *National Review,* July 14, 1997.

Wesley J. Smith   "Suicide in the West," *Weekly Standard,* April 20, 1998.
                    Available from News America Inc., 1211 Avenue of the
                    Americas, New York, NY 10036.

Sheryl Gay Stolberg "Assisted Suicides Are Rare, Survey of Doctors Finds,"
                    New York Times, April 23, 1998.

Earl Winkler   "Reflections on the State of Current Debate over
                    Physician-Assisted Suicide and Euthanasia," *Bioethics,*
                    July 1995. Available from Blackwell Publishers, 238 Main
                    St., Cambridge, MA 02142.

Index